Godforsaken Idaho

Godforsaken Idaho

STORIES

SHAWN VESTAL

NEW HARVEST
HOUGHTON MIFFLIN HARCOURT
Boston   New York
2013

This edition published by special arrangement with Amazon Publishing

For information about permission to reproduce selections from this book,
write to Permissions, Houghton Mifflin Harcourt Publishing Company,
215 Park Avenue South, New York, New York 10003.

www.hmhbooks.com

Library of Congress Cataloging-in-Publication Data
Vestal, Shawn.
Godforsaken Idaho : stories / Shawn Vestal.
pages cm
ISBN 978-0-544-02776-3 (pbk.)
1. Mormons — Fiction. I. Title.
PS3622.E875G63 2013
813'.6 — dc23
2012042644

Book design by Brian Moore

Printed in the United States of America
DOC 10 9 8 7 6 5 4 3 2 1

Stories in this collection have appeared in *Tin House, McSweeney's,
Ecotone, Quarterly West, The Southern Review, Montana Quarterly,
American Short Fiction, Filter, Real Unreal: The Best American Fantasy 3,*
and *Best of the West.*

For Amy

And if ye shall say there is no law, ye shall also say there is no sin. If ye shall say there is no sin, ye shall also say there is no righteousness. And if there be no righteousness there be no happiness. And if there be no righteousness nor happiness there be no punishment nor misery. And if these things are not there is no God. And if there is no God we are not, neither the earth; for there could have been no creation of things, neither to act nor to be acted upon; wherefore, all things must have vanished away.

— THE BOOK OF MORMON

Contents

Godforsaken Idaho

The First Several Hundred Years
Following My Death

THE FOOD IS EXCELLENT. The lines are never long. There's nothing to do with your hands. These are the first things I tell my son. Then we don't talk again for something like two hundred years.

The food is excellent, but nobody knows where it comes from. Your mother's Sunday dinner. A corn dog from the county fair. You eat from your own life only. You order from memory, as best you can. Your birthday cake, your wedding cake, your graduation barbecue. You give the cafeteria workers some coordinate, some connection, and out comes the tray. Your grandmother's pot roast. The double cheeseburger from the Lincoln Inn.

If you try to take a bite of someone else's food, it vanishes as your teeth descend.

In the cafeteria the workers call out the year at regular intervals. For a while, every time you go to eat you hear them shouting: "Twenty-five thirty-four! Twenty-five thirty-four!"

Until, before you know it: "Twenty-five thirty-five! Twenty-five thirty-five!"

Right now, as I tell this, it's 2613. There's a long way to go.

Your age at death becomes your age forever. Your body at death is your body forever — from scars to missing limbs to brain damage. In the cafeteria, people sit with others of their age and era — tables full of bald old men from my century, children from flu epidemics in the 1800s, young soldiers from every time. When you see mixed ages, it's a family, and it usually means someone new has arrived and they've gathered in welcome.

I woke up here at forty-seven, a familiar arthritic throb in my hip. I couldn't think what came before. I beat almost everyone: my mother, my two brothers, my son, my daughter, my ex-wife, possible grandchildren, and Janet, the woman who lived in the apartment down the hall. Not counting my father, I went first out of all the people who mattered in my life. I never went to a single funeral that made me cry.

After my ex-wife, Brynne, arrived and spent fifty years or so here, we talked about that. How I left so much grieving behind. She told me it was just one more example of me getting away with something. She was still angry, after all that time.

"You never wanted to do the things everybody had to do," she said. "You're like a child."

"No one's life is all one way," I said.

"Or an impulsive monkey."

In my whole life I never felt anything but thwarted and blocked. Nobody ever understands you, not even here.

Here is something I wish I'd told my son and never have: There is no peace here. All the trappings of peace, yes, all the silence and emptiness, but those are just shells. If you want peace, you have to find it in the life you left behind.

You wake in a simple room of interlocking cinder blocks, painted gray. One chair, one cot, one window filled with opaque gray. You can't tell whether the gray is outside air or the windowpane itself. You will never know. It is like morning, in half-light. A late morning after a dream.

That's all.

When I woke up here, Dad came to see me first — he showed me out of my room and explained how the cafeteria works. He called me "buddy" and seemed maniacally happy about my arrival.

"Wasn't expecting *you* this quick," he said, and then he laughed so wide I could see the metal fillings in his back teeth.

He was nervous, a lot nicer than I was used to. I'm older than him here, and that was strange. We stole looks at each other like kids at a dance. Pretty soon, my whole outlook on him changed. I'd always thought he was mean, but I started to see him as merely young, too young to expect much from. I hoped maybe I could teach him a thing or two, but nothing like that ever grew up between us.

I don't know why, but he never told me about reliving. I found out about that on my own.

A few decades later, my daughter, Annie, arrived and I started going to see her. She was too young to die — breast cancer at fifty-one — but she's older than me here. She seemed perfectly put together — neat black hair, big alert eyes, a stillness under every movement. I felt proud of her, though I had no credit coming. We would get together and share a meal, and I would try to give her advice about this place. I made a point of telling her about the reliving — how to control it, how to guide it.

"Now that it's gone," I said, "your life is the only thing you have left."

I told her how to concentrate in just the right way, to lock on to some detail or emotion from the moment in your life that you want to visit. Concentrate in the right way, I said, and the next thing you know, you're back in it. Back in it for as long as you want. Back in it to hunt for perfect moments. I told her to watch out for the bad times, though, how the bad times are always underneath even the happiest ones. I gave her the best advice I could. I was afraid she might be forgiving me in the same way I had forgiven Dad — holding me one or two percent less to blame due to my youth and ignorance.

"Try sports," I said, suggesting some avenues for reliving. "You always liked sports."

She was a nice woman, no thanks to me, so I didn't find out for years that she hadn't played a sport since she was twelve, that she never attended a sporting event as an adult, and that she refused to let her son play football because she was scared he would get hurt.

I am in the swimming pool, bob-walking through the shallow end, water tugging against me as I try to speed up, and the pool is a chamber of sound, of children's cries and parents calling and everybody shouting names, names, names, but none of them mine. I sink underwater and open my eyes in the stinging blue. It's like shade under there, legs like machine parts, moving without purpose against the pressure of silence.

It's hard to keep straight, but it goes something like this: My father died first, then me, then my mother, my ex-wife, my daughter, Janet from down the hall, my son.

Janet, the last woman in my life, the last chance at a real whatever, told me after she arrived that she didn't want to see me here. She was the first to turn. After I died, she'd started seeing a counselor. She said I had abused her emotionally.

"Emotional abuse is every bit as harmful as physical abuse," she said, nodding certainly. "Every bit."

"How would you know?" I said. "Even if I did abuse your

emotions? Did I ever hit you? Did anyone ever hit you? Physical abuse is probably *a lot* worse."

This was fairly early in my death. I hadn't yet begun to prize relationships.

She said, "You didn't love me enough. You didn't love me at all, maybe."

"I absolutely did," I said, which wasn't true, not like with my wife, who I loved so much at one time that I felt like it could have destroyed me. Janet and I drifted together thanks to drink and the proximity of our apartments. I hadn't been aware that love was even hovering around our hemisphere. I had always thought that was the good part about us.

The food is excellent. The lines are never long. You eat from your own life only. Once I sat by two men eating greasy squirrel, just gnawing it off a greenwood spit. Looking all Appalachian. They froze to stare over the tiny blackened limbs at a tall, good-looking dude walking by, all big hair and swagger.

"If that ain't Joe fucken Smith," one of them muttered, then went back to his squirrel angrily.

For me, though, the food is excellent.

You can order generally or specifically. It's fun to listen to the people around you as they order.

Hamburger, please. Any one from the Oh-So-Good Inn.

I'd like the prix fixe meal I had with my wife in Paris, 1961.

Easter ham and scalloped potatoes. Whenever.

Once he discovered the cafeteria, my son, Tyler, ate the

same thing for years and years. This was long after he'd arrived, and we'd started seeing each other occasionally.

"Thanksgiving dinner!" he would say, like he didn't know how loud he was being. And then he would shovel it in while I talked. I would ask him if he remembered this or remembered that, and he would nod like he was keeping time to a song. He was old, old enough to be my grandfather.

"You liked Thanksgiving, did you, Tyler?" I said once.

"I went by Reed," he said.

His middle name. His grandpa's name.

Here's what I should have told him, and what I still, for various reasons, have not: Now that it's gone, your life is the only thing you have left. Ransack it, top to bottom. Plunder that fucker. Find whatever you can in there, because it's all there is.

I am with Angela Jarvik in her bedroom and her parents are downstairs and we know that they never come up and she has her hand on me, over my jeans, and I have my hand on her, inside her jeans, and her mouth tastes like sweet metal and she groans and twists away. I am on my back in the sandy weeds outside the kegger, and Jennifer Luttin has me pinned, slides onto me, her kinky black hair brushing my face, and I feel an exquisite tightness beneath a flaming center, and when she leans forward to kiss me, I taste beer and cigarettes and see a burst of white. I am in the apartment of a woman named Sandy, who I met over Christmas break in

Boise, and she is whispering nastily in my ear while I'm just trying not to let it end too soon, and then I am on my knees on a hardwood floor at the foot of a bed, my face between the legs of my not-yet-wife, Brynne, and my tongue aches, and then I am in the shower with a woman whose name I can't remember, I'm behind her and she's leaning forward, and she's saying the filthiest things and I get all twisted up inside and thrust into her as hard as I can, like I want to hurt her, but she slips a little forward and then I do too, ramming my leg against the cold-water spigot, which leaves a stupendous bruise, a bruise that I know I will have to lie about to Brynne and then keep straight in my head what the lie was in case it somehow comes up again, now that I'm careful about every story.

You know it when the people you love die. You become aware. I first visited Brynne right after she arrived. I took myself to her room and waited outside her door until she opened it. When she saw me she flinched.

Her hair was white and thin. You could see through to her scalp. Liver spots covered her arms, and her heavy breasts made a stomach inside her smock. She seemed somewhat like the woman I had once loved, but thickened with sloughing latex and talc. I wanted to tug at the skin of her neck. I wanted to peel away the folds above her eyebrows.

"How do you feel?" I asked.

"Strange," she said.

"Can I come in?"

"I don't think so."

She seemed confused. She had to be eighty.

"You know I'm Rex," I said.

"I know who you are," she said.

I hadn't seen her for eleven years before I died. Now all I wanted was to find something beautiful in her, something that could remind me of her knockout twenty-three-year-old self. Then I thought, not for the first time: *I am a purely horrible person.* Her eyes were wet with anger.

"Are the kids all right?" I asked.

"You got used to not knowing that," she said.

"Come on," I said. "I've been dead."

I died lucky. You could go in a coma or after dementia. Some people never get out of their cots and make it to the cafeteria. You could go young, without enough to relive. Because that's everything, the reliving, the hunt for perfect moments. The poor kids, the teenagers, the twenty-year-olds — you look at them and they're beautiful, you want to taste them. The younger kids run screaming through the cafeteria, playing tag, and you think at least they've found something to do and a way to make friends. The games of tag include kids from everywhere, all times and places, African kids and Japanese kids and American kids and Bolivian kids. It is the only joy you ever see.

Sometimes you envy these children. Then you realize all

they'll never be able to relive, all the food they never ate, the places they never went, the sex they never had, the Christmas mornings, the Easter Sundays.

I am sitting on the couch in my bathrobe, and Brynne is cross-legged on the floor, helping Tyler and Annie open their gifts. The odor of evergreen and coffee fills the room. Charlie Brown Christmas music. Tyler throws his new football and it hits Annie in the face, bouncing into her Barbie Beach House, and she begins to howl. Brynne says, "Tyler," and he says, "I didn't mean to," but I know he's lying, and a surge runs through me and I vibrate with fury that we can't just have a simple fucking Christmas morning, kisses and hugs and then some football, and not a house full of crying and the smell of dirty clothes and bad breath. Tyler picks up the ball and spikes it like one of those NFL showboats and it bounces onto the coffee table and knocks my cup to the ground. I pick him up by his arm and swat him three times, hard on the butt. I only hear him bawling a few seconds later, after I've put him down and something has evaporated inside my head. Brynne shuffles up onto her knees and wraps him in her arm. She kneels there, one arm around each child. Looks at me without blinking. Packages wrapped in silver and red and green. Tyler cries louder than he needs to. Brynne keeps her eyes right on me. She hasn't blinked in forever.

Nobody tells you anything. No instruction sheet, no welcome wagon. You wake up on your cot. Your room is empty and pleasantly cool. Eventually you go out, where the balconies stretch in either direction, up and down, for farther than you can see. Across a gulf is another series of balconies, facing back, with precisely spaced doorways. The light is constant, institutional. At the bottom of the gulf is the cafeteria, filled with metal tables and chairs, welded to the gray concrete floor. Every few hundred yards is another line. The food is excellent. The lines are never long.

My father was the first to point this out. When he showed up at my door initially, he wanted to talk a lot, which seemed unusual. When we were growing up, he'd come home from work and the house would go silent for hours. Sometimes if he was watching TV and I started making too much noise, he would call out, "Shut it, Rex." If my mother was telling him a story, he'd interrupt before she finished and say, "Enough already."

Now he wants to talk.

We go to the cafeteria, and we try to order meals together. We pick Sundays out of a hat and see what we get. Chicken and potatoes. Roast beef with gravy. A lot of times we'll eat two in a row.

He asks me questions about my childhood, asks me didn't I think I was lucky to have the upbringing I did, wasn't our family one of the lucky ones, and because it's all over and doesn't matter, I say yes.

He always was an asshole, honestly. But he was a good provider. That was what Mom said, and once I became a father I thought that was what I was too. A good provider.

The head of the household. Later, after I'd vanished and left the household headless, I tried hard to remind myself how much I'd hated it whenever Dad was in the house, how the air grew thick with tension, how we held our laughter under our breath. How happy I thought we'd be if he would just leave.

At the cafeteria, people gather by age—tables of snowy-haired white people, tables of smiling, gabbing African children with protruding bellies. Kids race between the tables, squealing, and sometimes a crank will yell at them. You can recognize a killjoy in every language in the history of the world. Other children sit glumly by themselves, and they are a shattering sight, because you realize that the allure of tag, like everything, can last only so long.

I made friends with a guy from the Middle Ages. He died old for his day: forty-three. He loves to hear about televisions and microwave ovens. Tells the damnedest stories about the plague years, about the exhilaration of every day. When things got depressing, he and his friends would go out looking for Jews or lepers and beat them with clubs.

"The Black Death," he said, with an air of pride. "You knew you were alive. You knew the value of a day."

He slurped from his spoon, and his smile fell. "When my daughter got it, that was the worst. I'd have rather had it myself."

He looked around for eavesdroppers. We were sitting at the metal cafeteria tables. I was eating a corn dog from the

Ada County Fair, 1976. He was eating his wife's mutton stew, with salt and bread, from the winter of 1335.

He held his spoon poised between bowl and mouth. One cube of flabby mutton. He whispered, "I'd have rather my wife had it. I would have given it to her if I could've."

I remembered how worried we'd been when Tyler had the flu as a baby. The chemical purity of the hospital.

The man's eyes turned bright. "Tell me again about your toilet," he said. "You would sit there and read magazines."

My son sometimes eats four meals in a row. The same thing, four times in a row. He walks up to the counter and yells, "Thanksgiving dinner!" He is shiny on top, with blotchy brown freckles on his scalp, and his cheeks have slumped into jowls.

One time I told him, as he worked a huge forkful of turkey and mashed potatoes into his mouth, "I thought about you kids on the holidays every year. I really did. That might be part of what I had coming, I guess. I'm not asking for any slack, Tyler."

He chewed for fifteen seconds, then said, "Seriously. Nobody calls me Tyler, Ray."

"Rex," I said, feeling a knot of impossibility tightening. "Or you could call me Dad."

There is no peace here, and so you go looking in the life you left behind. You think it will be full of perfect moments — great days, great afternoons, great nights, a collection of moments that constitute a shorter, more perfect life. First you relive all the sex, then you try the peak days—the weddings, the births of your children, the graduations. Then sports and hobbies, then work, then your kids' school plays. You remember something that seemed good and you go back to it.

But you find it hard to land in a single untroubled moment. Every second is crowded with life, with misery and anxiety that just won't be stomped down. Even the happiness can kill you. I went back for the birth of my son, and it shocked me how disfiguring it was, all that intensity, how it broke me open in a way that soared way beyond happiness.

The door at The Mirage lets in a slab of yellow light. A woman comes in, fortyish. Tattoo on a freckled bosom. Can't tell yet what it is. Smoker's laugh. I am at the bar, four hours in. It is cool and drunk. I am cool and drunk. I turn a pack of matches in my fingers, folding and unfolding the cover. I want to climb that woman. I light a cigarette and watch her, raising my eyebrows and holding out the pack, and she accepts. Janet. We tell our stories in the dark. The world is full of hope, and mistakes are easy to spot. We're at her apartment by eight thirty. When I kneel to tug down her pilled satiny panties, I notice curly hairs escaping from the homeland between her legs, little strays on the pillowy inside of her thighs.

· · ·

The first time I saw my son here, he seemed confused, like Brynne had. Then I relived a bunch of the old times I'd had with him, and my self-loathing became richer, developed shades and nuance. Even the safest-seeming times roiled with undertow. We played catch in the backyard, and I yelled at him for throwing wild. I taught him how to ride a bike. When he fell over and skinned his knee, I mocked him for crying. I wanted him to be tough.

And then, back here, I couldn't make myself go see him again for a long, long time.

I relived the first years of my marriage. Some days I relived morning to night, over and over again. Hardly any undertow.

Then I'd come back here, where I hate the way my ex-wife is now. I longed for the young her everywhere, and the only way I could get her off my mind was to bury myself in diversionary reliving. I repeated four hours drunk at The Mirage with my buddies Kevin and Jayce thirteen times in a row. I went to a Foghat concert, Boise, 1972. One week I spent in Belize with my college girlfriend, mostly on a king bed with the balcony door open to a perfect blue seam of sky and sea. The small, cocoa-colored man at the hotel's front desk smiled shyly at us whenever we passed. We did it in the shower, in a chair, with her leaning out over the balcony in the middle of the night. I held her from behind, felt her ribs in my hands.

Every time I came back here, I was ravenous. In the cafeteria, I ordered the Belize meals again — whole red snapper, pit-roasted pig, bottles of clear Belikin beer. I would sit there and eat slowly, watch the children at tag, and feel a tender ache in my balls and long for sunburn and the whispery feel of dried seawater on my skin.

After Brynne showed up here, we started seeing each other from time to time. She softened. I wondered when my children might appear. She told me about their lives. Tyler was a train wreck: married, had a son, divorced, went to jail, his ex died, took the kid back, messed that up something awful. Eventually, he lived alone in Denver, and almost never called. Annie had married a guy who used her good credit to buy cars and a home, and then ruined it before she knew what was happening. Spent money like crazy. They had two children, a boy and a girl, and Annie decided to stay with him even after they had to turn their house over to the bank and rent an apartment.

"Did they ever ask about me?" I asked her.

"All the time," she said.

"What'd you tell them?"

"I told them how we met. I told them about the day we got married. How handsome you were. How hard you worked. How no one could understand the way you just vanished. How you still loved them."

"Wow," I said. "I don't know what to say."

"How it was probably hard for you to live with what you'd done."

All I'd done, at first, was the usual rigmarole. Sleeping around. All that urgency about women. Your whole life concentrated into tiny waves and crests. We had a teary day when Brynne found out, a day I found myself dragged back to repeatedly when I wasn't careful about reliving. She told me I didn't deserve to have a family anymore. The kids watched us fight like they were peering through a fence at barking dogs. I moved into a room downtown, and within a week she and the kids had moved to her mother's in Oregon.

I've spent years trying to figure out why I did what I did next. I didn't call the kids for eight months, and then, after fourteen minutes on the telephone, I didn't talk to them again for four years. They sent a few letters at first.

"How you probably hated yourself," she said. "And who could blame you?"

I am driving home to Gooding from Twin Falls on I-84 when the semitruck in front of me begins to change lanes and slides sideways on a patch of ice. It stretches out before me, then I hit the ice myself, and when the semi reaches the next dry patch it crashes onto its side, sparking off the freeway and into the snowy weed chaff alongside the road and ramming a power-line pole. I slide off, roll once, and come to rest. The world goes silent. Something cloudy in my head. Adrenaline racing. Trembling.

I think of the kids.

I think, *OK, Rex.*

I open the door and step out and a surge of unbelievable

whiteness passes through me, shoots out my eyes and fingertips.

January 13, 1979.

Then I woke up here. I always wanted to know more about it, see my funeral, see the days after, watch how my void took shape. Like Tom Sawyer at his funeral. But you don't get to do that.

Eventually, you give up on finding the shorter, more perfect life. You start hunting for a single great day. One day of peace. One day of still water, start to finish. Then, after a few years, you start to think: OK, one great afternoon. One morning.

One great hour.

Ecstatic moments lose their thrill. The worst times start feeling attractive. Everything pressed to the edge, pulled into focus.

I stumbled across a day right after my wife had her miscarriage. It came between our kids, late in the pregnancy. A humid oppression over everything. Everywhere we looked, we saw babies — mothers carrying red-faced infants, strollers crowding the sidewalks.

One day we were watching TV and a diaper commercial came on, with a peach-colored infant sitting on a white backdrop.

I said, "Jesus Christ. We ought to make a drinking game of it."

Brynne began to cry and wouldn't let me touch her.

Her tears didn't move me much. That's not the way I wish I had been, but I have to say it. Nothing felt important.

Later that night, after she'd gone to bed, I sat on our front steps. It was summer, the nights cool, and as I sat there, a skinny gray and orange cat came into our yard and looked at me. The cat seemed hungry and shrill, alone, and it mewled at me. I looked away. The cat made the sound again, more keenly, with more ache, and then wandered off.

My eyes burned.

When I came back here, I developed an unbelievable longing for a cat, a desire to hold a cat in my lap or scratch one between the ears, and the emptiness of the days became defined by catlessness.

Once, for what felt like a hundred years, I became obsessed with cigarettes. I found myself reliving ten minutes of smoking from 1977, perched on a stool at The Mirage Lounge, over and over again. It was like smoking thirty-seven cigarettes in a row and then emerging with clear lungs. And then lying around and eating meals and longing for the cancerous bite of the smoke in your chest, yearning for it like you were yearning for the return of your one great love, and all you can feel the entire time is desire, which bleeds the reliving paler and paler with each turn. Sometimes you need to sleep for a long time afterward. It's really the only time you can sleep, when you've relived something exhausting, and when you return, sadness follows you around like a dog you want to kick, and so you sleep for a long, long time, until your hunger forces you awake.

My son died at ninety-three. He went in his sleep, which made me happy. I went right to his door. The sight of him shocked me. A distorted version of me — larger in every particular: head, hands, frame, nose. And yet his whole body cramped down, hands gathered inward like claws. He looked like he was still dying.

"Tyler, it's your dad," I said, and he said, "OK."

"You remember me, don't you?"

He worked his mouth for a second, and said, "You seem like someone."

He fixed his eyes on the wall somewhere behind me, and I left. For two hundred years or so I thought about that moment the most. You can drive yourself crazy. I don't know what made me go back, besides having enough time to think it over.

Tyler seemed the same when his door opened to me a second time. I went in and sat on the chair, and then he sat on the cot. He waited.

"I've been thinking about you a lot, son. Thinking about you and me, and realizing how much I let you down. You and your sister. And your mother, of course."

He nodded absently. He sat forward in his chair, and his head bobbed.

"I know I wasn't much of a father. I know that. But I hope we can work back to something together. All of us. We're

still a family, you know, no matter how much hurt we've suf-
fered."

He cleared his throat, and seemed to wait for a few seconds to make sure I was done. I couldn't read anything in his
face.

"I don't go in for a lot of talk," he said.

We sat in silence for what must have been an hour, until I
said, "Are you hungry?" and he said, "I don't have any food."

"What about the cafeteria?"

He looked at me blankly. I became aware of the possibility that he had not yet left his room, after all these years. I
walked to his door, then out to the balcony, and looked back
at him. He sat unmoving for several moments, and then I
said, "Come on."

He came uncertainly onto the balcony. Brittle on his feet.
He looked carefully out and down into the chasm.

"What is this place?" he asked.

I had been dead for 326 years when I got an idea. We would
have a family dinner. Me, Tyler, Brynne, and Annie. When
I told Brynne, she said Annie would want to bring her husband. I'd never met him. And their kids. My grandchildren.

"And why not my parents?" she said.

"And mine?" I said.

Brynne made a face. She'd never liked my folks. She was
from Boise people. Golfers who dressed nice and acted nervous around me. Smiley and fake. My dad milked cows for
other men. We'd lived in Eden, didn't even have a post office.

"Look, if we're going to invite everybody, we can't go leaving out my family," I said.

"I don't see why not," Brynne said.

"Maybe I should invite one of my girlfriends," I said, and here's maybe one thing about me that's different now: I knew that was shitty the moment I said it. Used to be, when I said some shitty, mean thing, I justified it to myself for days and days, until I realized that it was shitty and told myself I'd never do it again. Now, I recognized it immediately. It was a hopeful sign. There's a long way to go.

I told my friend from the Middle Ages about my plan for a family dinner.

"That sounds awful," he said.

"Why?"

"I'm sick of this food. I'm sick of eating the same thing every day forever. I'm sick of old lamb. I'm sick of potatoes and mush cakes. You know what I did? I went back and ordered the gruel we ate during the winter of 1329, when we were damn near starving, and the soup had got rotten and it made us all so sick we almost died. I laid about in bed, shitting myself until I couldn't shit again. Days of that. I thought I was going to die. My wife crying all the time, begging God, this and that." He laughed. "We didn't know what we had then, is what it is. We had no idea what we had."

"I guess not."

"So here, I go up and order that rotten soup and eat it, and you know what happens?"

"What?"

"Nothing."

"That's good."

He looked at me in disgust, and spat a piece of bone into his bowl.

It's hard to get a group together. There's no way to communicate — if you want to see someone, the only thing to do is go and see them. So Brynne and I split up and went door-to-door. Brynne went to get her family. I went first to Tyler's.

"You want to have what kind of dinner?" he asked.

Tyler and I went to Annie's.

"I guess, if Reed's coming," she said.

Tyler, Annie, and I went to see Annie's husband, Duff. He looked pretty good — he'd come here at fifty-eight. Heart attack.

Then Tyler, Annie, Duff, and I went to see Duff and Annie's kids. When I introduced myself, they had looks of uncertainty in their eyes. Like they'd forgotten the details, but remembered the general idea.

We all went to see my mother. She wept a little when I told her what we were doing.

"Oh, Rex," she said. "I always knew you were a good boy."

Then we went to see my dad.

"Sounds like a lot of noise and trouble, buddy," he said, and the words filled me with a painful nostalgia for childhood.

Brynne went around to her people, too. And they went

wild. Shook the whole family tree, back through the generations. By the time we arrived at the cafeteria, the lines were outrageous at every station, and all of them, somehow, supposedly, tied back to us. The branches of my tree, the Todd family, and Brynne's, the Warrens, stretching backward and forward in time.

Right away, I saw how lame this would be. It wasn't going to work at all. I had envisioned something shared, a real family meal, I don't know why, but Brynne was over in a different line with her folks, who nodded at me coolly, and Annie and her husband were way behind me in my line, and I saw others walking away from the stations with all different kinds of food — stews and charred hunks of meat and mush with butter and tacos and potatoes of every shape and nature, from French fried to mashed to baked to whatever. One lumpy guy shuffled past holding a tray with four enormous, identical bowls of Neapolitan ice cream. A striking, large-eyed young woman with a single braid of dark hair carried a tray mounded with Christmas stockings, spilling out oranges and peanuts and hard candy.

I was standing with Tyler and his son, my grandson, an old man named Zachary, who was talking on and on about the family tree. Zachary was thin and frail, and spoke with a careful precision, as though he were being recorded. He'd converted to Mormonism during his life, then become fascinated with genealogy.

"You might be surprised to know," he said, all playful and

smug in a way that I already hated, "that you and Grandma are actually related, if you go back far enough."

"Yeah?" I asked. It was hard, still, to think of me and Brynne as grandparents. "How far back is far enough?"

Zachary looked at me in the assessing way, the withholding way that Brynne's parents always used — like they were expressing a tolerance for my very existence. He looked at me in that way, and also with a kind of mischief, as though he could not wait to tell me this thing that he thought was so important, this paltry fact about who gave birth to whom all those impossible years ago.

"Your great-great-grandmother is her great-great-*great* grandmother!" he said.

"Fascinating," I said, and stepped up to place my order: the rib eye with mushrooms and garlic mashed potatoes from Diamondfield Jack's in Twin Falls, 1978, a meal from a date with Janet, not too long before the day of my death.

We sat down, Tyler, Zachary, and I, and started eating. Zachary introduced me to some of the others there, but I soon stopped paying attention. I looked around, at the tables full of strangers spilling in every direction and tried to estimate how many people were there. Hundreds, easily. Though it was impossible to tell exactly where our crowd ended and the line of other, unrelated people began. I tried to find some family feeling inside myself for all these strangers, and could not, but I noted the return of something I remembered from life: the sense that these people, all these people I was knotted to without choice, would steal my life and harness it to theirs.

"There she is," Zachary said, pointing to the beautiful young woman with the long braid, sitting before the tray of oranges and Christmas stockings. "That's her."

I crammed an enormous piece of steak in my mouth and chewed. Tyler did the thing he always did, loading a fork with a piece of turkey, a glob of mashed potatoes and a bit of stuffing.

"Sara Warren," Zachary said. "The one I was talking about."

When I merely stared at him, chewing, he said, "Your ancestor, and your wife's."

"Wonderful," I said.

He giggled. I considered flipping a mushroom at him with my spoon.

I said, "Isn't the food here wonderful?"

Zachary looked at me like I was insane.

That was when I realized. The food here is not excellent. That's just a lie. It's the same food, the same food, the same food forever.

That was the last one, that family dinner. If the rest of them are getting together, they're not inviting me.

You finally find it, and it's not even an hour.

For me, it lasts thirteen minutes and forty-seven seconds. I stand on a bridge and look into the Snake River Canyon.

It's two weeks after Brynne kicked me out. I hear the wind sound of planes. The air smells like sweet hay and cow shit. My mind hums. I light one cigarette off another and watch the butt tumble out of sight into the canyon below. I am entirely alone. The emptiness makes a sound that takes in everything.

About as Fast as This Car Will Go

I NEVER WANTED TO BE a criminal until I was one. And then, for a while, I couldn't imagine wanting to be anything else.

I was seventeen when Dad got out of prison for the second time. Aunt Fay didn't want me to go back to him. "Stay," she told me, fanning out community college brochures on the Formica table. "Finish your school."

For two years, she and Uncle Mitch had been great — everything open-door, come and go, free access to the fridge, a place of my own in the basement. Mitch worked at the seed company, and Fay baked bread and fried doughnuts at Safeway. They liked to drink beer on the couch or head down to The Mirage to play pool and listen to the same songs on the jukebox.

Then Fay woke up New Year's Day with a huge bruise on her hip that she couldn't remember how she got. It was spectacular — a saddle around her side, back, and stomach, purple-blue and wavy at the edges, yellow and red in the middle.

Mitch said, "Search me."

That morning I'd woken up before everybody else, gotten a box of Count Chocula, and sat on the couch with the TV on, eating by the handful in my underwear and T-shirt. Fay came out at noon, dream-logged and slow. She was poking at her side and wincing when she saw me. She stood in the frame of the hall, and her guilty look made me ashamed.

After that, Fay always wanted to know where I was going and how I was doing in school. She quit drinking. She cut her hair short. When Dad's release date started getting close, she talked to me about staying put and finishing school, about stability, the importance of education.

"Look at this, Zach," she said one night, turning the glossy pages on the community college brochures. "You can train for all kinds of good jobs."

She wore her Safeway smock and smelled of fryer grease. She flipped pages on programs to become a diesel mechanic, a licensed practical nurse, a computer programmer. I looked at the brochures, with the smiling students taking a temperature or probing a truck engine, and tried to picture myself in that world, getting smarter and earning money, falling in love and living in a house like a real person. Fay was so hung with expectation that I told her OK, but I never thought we were talking about anything real. I figured her for two or three months on the straight and narrow until something glassy showed in her eyes again.

Dad wore the same thing coming out he wore going in: jeans, snap-button shirt, cowboy boots. His clothes seemed hangy and big, like he'd shrunk inside them, and his sideburns were turning gray.

We drove to Boise to pick him up in his own car, the slouching, soft-shocked Pontiac. Mitch drove, guiding us in and out of the passing lane, and Fay talked and talked. I stretched my legs out on the back seat, sick with nerves, but then we saw him and he was just Dad, and he hugged me and joked around and called me kiddo.

"You're getting *huge*," he said, like he hadn't seen me two months before. He and Fay and Mitch all laughed at this, my unbelievable growth. Fay had us stand back-to-back and said I had him by an inch. "Stop it already," he said.

In the car Fay talked about where to go for lunch. Dad said he'd heard about a good Basque place from one of the guys in his anger-management sessions.

"Embezzler," he said, and laughed. "Angry embezzler."

We ate lamb stew and chorizo and spicy potatoes and thick soup, drinking it all down with red wine. Dad ate two of everything, wiped his bread around the curve of his bowl and smiled while he chewed. Mitch rambled on about Y2K, the upcoming computer apocalypse, and Dad pretended to listen. Afterward we went to the park by the river and Dad kneeled and ran his hands over the cold grass, put his face down and breathed it in, and then he lay on it, face down. He turned over on his back, eyes closed, smiling.

On the way home he sprawled on the seat beside me, so relaxed he seemed ready to come apart completely.

"Must be great to be out," I said.

"It's all right," he said, opening his eyes and looking away.

Months later we picked up the man in the tan suit at the diner. We drove him into the desert. He was trying to get home to see his daughter in Boise. He'd left her and her mother years ago, left and never went back. He was afraid she'd never forgive him.

"Nothing more important than family," Dad said. "She's got to realize that."

I had no friends then. Not one. I knew people, and I'd had friendships here and there, but something always broke them up. Mostly we'd just gradually stop being friends, the way we'd gradually started. When my seventeenth birthday came, a couple months before Dad got out, Mitch, Fay, and I went to Café Olé in Twin Falls, where the waiters come out and sing and put a sombrero on you and take a Polaroid. Fay told me I could bring a friend, but I couldn't think of anyone. We'd lived in Gooding all our lives.

In the picture, Fay is poised, arm around my shoulder. Mitch gazes out of the frame. My face is hidden by the shadow of the sombrero. If you saw it, you'd think: mother, father, son.

On the way home from Boise that first day, Fay worked herself up and turned around and told Dad she thought I should stay with her and Mitch, at least until I finished school.

Dad tipped his head — like, *maybe* — and chewed the inside of his lip.

Fay said it would just be for stability, so I could get through classes without disruption. I was three months from graduation. Class of Double Zero. She told him about the community college, the mechanics program, the bright future, and common sense.

"Well," he said finally, "I guess I just figured I'd have my boy with me."

My blood raced. Nobody spoke for the longest time.

"You're not exactly set up to be a parent right now, Reed," Fay said. "Forgive my saying."

Mitch said, "Fay."

Dad didn't say anything. I held my breath, afraid I'd be asked to decide.

The man in the tan suit said he was trying to get to Boise to see his daughter. He hadn't seen her in twelve years. She was flying in from Oregon. He smelled like the front part of a department store, glass cases and glass bottles, chemical sweet. He'd moved to Idaho and taken another job and bought a house and met another woman.

"Like that other life hadn't ever been," he said.

Dad drove us down the freeway. He kept smiling at the man, tapping his hands on the steering wheel. I sat with my legs out on the back seat. We'd put our last seven dollars into the gas tank.

The man told us bits at a time. He had been driving to Boise from Twin Falls, going to pick up his daughter at the airport, when his car broke down. The mechanic needed a day to get the part, but that airplane from Oregon was on its way.

There was something utterly unbelievable about him, and yet I felt he was telling us the truth.

My father kept looking at me, his icy green eyes framed in the rearview mirror. He might have been mad at me, still. Or trying to communicate something. But there was nothing that perfect between us, no secret eye language of family.

The muscle beneath his left eye quivered, and he placed a finger on it, held it in place until it stopped.

When I was eleven, I watched Dad drag a teenager from his car in the parking lot at the swimming pool, shouting so loud a lifeguard came out to break it up.

"I'm going to kick your ass up between your shoulder blades," Dad shouted as he backed away. "You'll have to take off your shirt to take a shit."

The guy had been taunting me and Bucky Torr, a neighbor kid who'd come swimming with me. We were standing in our wet suits, wrapped in towels, on the lawn outside the pool. He'd called us pussies, dared us to grab the tits of the girls nearby. Bucky was about to cry, and when Dad pulled up and asked him what was wrong, he told him.

Watching my father, I could see it all happening, even though I couldn't tell you what it was. Something widened in his pupils and his nostrils. His face filled with blood. Then the door was swinging open, and we jumped out of the way.

Dad rented us an apartment downtown, above the Lincoln Inn. He got a job milking and lost it three days later, when the owner found out he'd been in prison. The guy said if Dad had only been honest, he might have kept him on.

"No way," Dad told me.

He started working the swing shift at Quik Mart, coming home afterward and telling me to go to bed. He asked about school, tried to keep the fridge full. He seemed nervous and dry-mouthed all the time. It was almost two weeks before they let him go.

He went to visit his parole officer in Twin Falls, and came back agitated.

"Like I haven't already had two jobs," he said. "Like I'm just sitting here."

He started staying out later, and then he vanished for two days. I stayed home, skipping school and waiting. I thought maybe I was already alone and just didn't know it yet, like he'd crashed that Pontiac and died but nobody knew to find me and tell me. I thought if that was true maybe I'd just stay still forever, inside the gray bubble of those days, and stop pretending there were other people for me.

He came back with a little money, said he'd found work roofing in Idaho Falls and meant to call, etc. We went downstairs for burgers. He had three beers with dinner, and he stayed in the bar when I came up and went to bed.

The next morning, a Thursday, I walked down the hall and saw Dad sprawled out on his bed, on top of the covers in his clothes. Everything was gray-lit and quiet. I walked back down the hall and climbed into bed. And that was it for school.

The day we met the man in the tan suit, we were out of money, angry, quiet. In a diner with vinyl seats, looking out a plate-glass window onto the Snake River. The man came in, looked around, walked over and offered to pay us for a ride to Boise.

"What do you think — twenty bucks?" he asked. "Thirty?"

He wore a tie, neat as a banker. He carried a deep maroon briefcase. He smelled nicer than the men I knew, and his eyes seemed loose and watery on his face. I could probably remember his name if I had to. It was just him and us in there, not counting the waitress and the cook.

"We're going that way," Dad said. "Buy our coffee, and we'll call it good."

I scooted over and the man sat down.

"I've got money," he said. He took a worn envelope from his briefcase, thick with bills, and slid out a twenty.

Dad wouldn't hear of it. He never looked at the money, but it seemed he was smelling it or tasting it. A blush high on his cheeks, and a spasm under one eye.

When Dad's parole officer knocked, announcing himself from the hallway — "Reed? It's Barrett Rudman. Open up" — I was both surprised and not, because some part of fearing is expecting. Dad motioned me into the bedroom and closed the door behind me.

I heard the man say he'd had a report that Dad had been drinking in a bar.

Dad asked who'd said that, and the man said it didn't matter, was it true, and Dad said no.

"If it is, I don't have to tell you what that means," the man said.

Dad said he hadn't been in a bar since his parole. He said he'd been working construction jobs, day work, and gave the name of a contractor to check with. He said he spent a lot of time with his boy, Zach, who lived with his aunt Fay and uncle Mitch.

He was an excellent liar. Really good. But it sounded like the parole officer didn't believe him. He told Dad to be careful. He said, "I'll be stopping by again."

Dad said fine, good, look forward to it. After the man left, Dad said, "That fucking Fay," and he went into the kitchen, opening and closing cupboards, slamming things, and then again, "That goddamned fucking Fay."

Dad disappeared again. For two days I went back to thinking he'd died without me knowing, or some other bad thing, but by the third day, when the food ran out, I knew he'd just left and wouldn't ever be back, and that Fay had been right all along.

That afternoon I walked to her house. She and Mitch were both at work. I walked through the back door and went right to the box of Quaker Oats in the cupboard where Fay hid her spending money. Thirty-four bucks. I went through the cupboards and the drawers. In the hallway closet, I grabbed Mitch's binoculars. In the bedroom, I took Fay's Walkman and some jewelry that wasn't worth a thing. I found sixty bucks hidden under some socks in Mitch's drawer.

I walked around. I wondered what other valuables there were, but everything seemed too cheap or too big or too worn out. On the fridge Fay had the picture of us at Café Olé, and another one of her and me, hung by magnets. I wanted to do more, something to show I'd been there, to say hello and fuck you, to say none of you get me now, but I couldn't think of a single thing.

At the grocery store I bought eggs, ham, and bread. I ate the same kind of sandwich four meals straight. Dusk drifted through the apartment. It felt like I might never see another person. I kept the blinds down. I looked over the jobs in the *Gooding County Leader* and wondered how you tried to get one.

It was noon and Dad was drunk when he came back, wobbly and smiling to himself. "Hey, kiddo," he said when he walked in.

I didn't answer.

"Come on, now," he said, slumping onto the couch and throwing an arm around me. "Don't be like that. I found a little work."

I watched the TV.

"In Boise. Hanging drywall."

When I didn't answer, his smile fell. He took his arm back and went into the kitchen, banging around until he came back with a bottle of Jack Daniel's and a glass. He poured himself about six fingers. He watched me steadily between gulps.

I fixed my eyes on the TV screen.

"Fine," he said, and carried his glass back into the kitchen. When he came back, he said, "Hey," and threw his car keys at me.

"Come on," he said. "You're driving."

I drove us to the outskirts of town, and he had me park on the shoulder, across the street from a gravel cul-de-sac rimmed with Boise Cascade homes stamped from the same blueprint. A blue one, a brown one, a yellow one. Windows all dark. People out living. He shushed me when I started to speak, and we sat there for twenty minutes.

Then Dad rubbed his hands on his jeans like he was trying to get feeling back in his fingers. He said, "I want you to promise you'll never tell anyone about this." He said, "You've got to listen to everything. Listen, listen, listen. Ask yourself what every sound is." He said, "We run at the first sign of trouble. There's plenty of time if you don't wait for things to get worse."

We walked down the lane, swishing through ditch weeds to avoid the noisy gravel, and came to a small house with a big fence toward the only neighbor. No dog barked. We circled behind and watched the back door.

He said, "Usually, the back door's best. I bet you a hundred bucks that back door's open, and if it's not, the next twenty-five will be." He said, "When you get in, stand absolutely still for twenty or thirty seconds. Listen."

We were going in there. I never had a doubt. I was high on it.

The man in the tan suit kept thanking us. I watched Dad's eyes in the mirror and wondered what we were doing. The money radiated through the car.

"A lot of people wouldn't just help a stranger like this," the man said. "Not like they used to."

"Don't give it another thought," Dad said.

We'd have to work for days to fill an envelope like that.

"For all you know, I could be a dangerous man. On the lam."

"You don't seem the type," Dad said, eyes in the mirror.

"Some kind of scumbag," the man said.

The color climbed Dad's neck.

Inside that first house, Dad motioned for me to stand still in the kitchen. He walked to drawers and opened them slowly. In one, he found a checkbook, which he lifted and pointed to, nodding and smiling. He put it back. He walked into the living room, looking back at me every so often, lifting objects and replacing them, opening doors, nudging things on the tables, showing me how silently he could move through absent lives. He put everything back, that time. He'd never steal anything that close to home.

Except, as we left, he picked up a cookie jar from the counter and tucked it under his arm. It was a ceramic French pig. You took off its beret to get at the cookies. We ate some in the car on the way back home. Store-bought.

Dad put the pig in the center of the kitchen table, and we ate all the cookies in two days. That jar sat there for three months, though it never held another cookie. It was where we kept the money. We'd take off in the Pontiac for a week to the podunk Mormon towns around Salt Lake, come back with checkbooks and new clothes and rolls of cash. We'd head to Helena and come back with a trunk load of shotguns to pawn.

The cookie jar was always full. Dad would buy us beer and we'd get drunk. He'd coach me on the finer points. We played cards and ate steak four times a week. I never got up in the morning, and never worried about getting to bed. I never had a moral qualm, I'm sorry to say. It was too much damn fun. Too much adrenaline and freedom. Me and my dad, money in the pig, nowhere to be.

We were sitting on the couch after dusting off a twelve-pack one night when he told me my hairline was receding. I reached up to feel it.

"No," I said.

"Yes, sir," he said. "It's starting."

Dad had a widow's peak, an isthmus of hair with deep recessions at the temples. I began checking my forehead carefully in the mirror, and some days I thought he was right and some days wrong. I liked the thought at first, the idea that there might be some physical evidence connecting us. Then it started seeming like the start of something unstoppable.

At some point Dad went to the pig and found six dollars. He crashed into my bedroom and started shoving things around on my dresser.

"What happened to all the money?" he said.

I was in bed, waking up. He opened drawers, clawed through my clothes. "You took some out," he said.

"Knock it off," I said. "There's no money in there. I might have a few bucks in my pants pocket, but that's it."

He picked up my pants and pulled out three crumpled ones. His eyes slid around in his twitchy face.

"Dad, come on."

He left for the rest of the day. That night he sat next to me on the couch and slapped me on the knee a couple times. He said we'd take off for Boise in the morning to fill up the pig.

"Hey, kiddo, I'm sorry about earlier. I was just surprised, is all."

I kept looking at the TV.

"Come on, Zach. You know I love you."

The next day we met the man in the tan suit and gave him a ride and learned all about his failed first life and his happy second life, and how he planned to make things right and how he hoped his daughter could forgive him. She was nineteen. Someone had cut out her wedding announcement and mailed it to him. When he saw it, he tracked her down and called her. Bought her a plane ticket.

"I left them in my dark days," he said. "I left them all alone. I'm afraid she'll never forgive me." We were driving on the freeway to Boise, windows down, the sweet dusty odor of hay on the rushing air. We turned off at Mountain Home. Dad told the man he had to swing by a friend's place, and then he drove deep into the desert, following county roads until they turned to gravel. He found a place beside a stand of trees.

"Got to see a man about a horse," he said, and then he yawned big, stretched his arms wide, and while the man looked outside, unafraid, Dad dropped his right arm, looked at me in the back seat like he was sending a message, and pointed at the bag sitting on the floor beside me.

I thought it was a big mistake, but I had no language for that. I reached into the bag.

Dad said, "Look for cash. Things that are small and valuable. Jewelry. Some kinds of knives. Binoculars." He said, "Don't shit where you eat. My rule is nothing closer than a hundred miles from home." He said, "Sometimes I think this is a mistake, what we're doing." He said, "Now you try it." He said, "Just squeeze." He said, "Sometimes I think this is the best life ever. I think of those people sound asleep right now, alarm clocks and ties and shit, and I think if you can just keep this going, it's the luckiest thing ever." He said, "If your mother could see this, God rest her, I'd catch hell." He said, "You know I love you, kiddo." He said, "Sir, we're gonna have to take that briefcase." He said, "All right now, sir, hand over that case or my boy will shoot you." He said, "We won't have any choice." He said, "Jesus Christ, Zach. Hold it like you mean it."

Families Are Forever!

GINA SAID, "I'D LOVE TO stab you to death with an ice pick. Like four hundred times." She feigned delicate stabs. "Or a hat pin." We were driving from Jackson to Rupert, Idaho, where her parents lived. An eight-hour drive. She'd already come up with: suffocation in a vat of excrement; poisoning with lye in cake frosting; crucifixion with rusty nails; and countless variations involving the mutilation of my genitals.

I said, "I'd cover you with some kind of bitter nectar, like concentrate of unripe guava, and stake you out in a Brazilian jungle for insects to devour."

Gina said, with a dash of mockery, "Devour."

Her parents lived on a farm that made me laugh when I first saw it: a cube of a white house, a green roof, a cement stoop, green shutters, a pine tree in the yard, and a field of what I thought was wheat surrounding it all. It was barley.

Flag on a pole. Norman Rockwell painted this, I thought, because it comes from nowhere real.

Going through Yellowstone, we got jammed up behind a line of cars. People crowded the shoulders of the road. I rolled down our window and asked a man what was happening.

"Bear," he said, hypercasual, all Davy Crockett. His blue-white legs stuck out of khaki shorts. "Griz."

He pointed to a smudge of golden brown on the hillside. It looked like a plant or a rock, and then it moved.

"Want a closer look?" he asked, holding out binoculars.

I put the glasses up and focused until the landscape came into view. I saw the bear, crashing pigeon-toed through the brush and stripping branches. Slobber fell from its wet, black mouth.

"Hon?" I said, offering the glasses.

She took them and peered through silently. She said quietly, "I'd like to tie you up and drag you out to that bear. Cover you with camper garbage."

She handed back the glasses. She flashed me a radiant smile, and I was stabbed by love. She thought I'd spent the $500 we owed her folks on ski passes, but I'd spent that money on other things and lied. We had fourteen bucks left in the checking account, and we were making the trip on our gas station credit card, watching for Shell signs everywhere.

We came out of Yellowstone, everything gradually flatter and tanner until we hit Idaho Falls, where we stopped at a Shell station for hot dogs and corn chips.

I was road-worn and smelly. "You want to drive?" I asked. She said, kind of loud, "Nope."

A few more hours and we'd be there. I thought how easy it was to spend $500. How big a difference there was between having $500 and knowing it was spoken for, and having $467 and knowing you can't pay the $500 anyway and what the hell. Here's the way it went: four nights with my friends, buying rounds; new speakers for the car stereo; coffees and lunch out every day. It was free fall. In high-school physics, old Mr. Lampert had illustrated gravity problems with chalkboard drawings of a stick man tumbling off a building. *When the falling man hits the earth, how fast will he be moving? What force will the falling man exert on the earth?* Spending that money was exhilarating. We'd scraped by since moving to Jackson, and I'd forgotten what it felt like to have a little money in your pocket. When Gina realized the money was gone, I made up the ski story on the spot. Which is always a mistake. Gina told me it was a betrayal, like an affair.

In the car, like she was reading my mind, she said, "The problem is, you don't really want to kill me. But I really, really want to kill you."

When we got there, Gina's mom and dad waited on the front step, shading their eyes against the low sun. On the lawn, off to the side, stood a little boy. I don't know, eight or ten. We don't have kids, and neither do our friends. Whenever I see them, I feel like I'm remembering something. Like childhood is something only from the past. The boy looked filmed with dirt, hair like the scuffy end of a hay bale.

Her mom rushed us, hugging and murmuring, while her dad hung back, waved and smiled — or maybe he didn't smile. Maybe he squinted. Gordon and Betty. Nice people. Salt of the earth, etc. Nothing like Gina. I tried to imagine her living there and could never do it. Like the whole Mormon childhood thing was made up, and she was born at age twenty-one, having already read the Bible and the Book of Mormon and put those aside, having already heard every good band and seen every good movie, so sarcastic she could kill you.

Betty was asking us about our drive, hoping it was all right, hugging and patting and smiling. A refusal to be weary. Thank you, Lord, may I have another. Gordon, who probably did less work, was always letting you know how tired he was with grunts and sighs and a hand on his back.

The boy stood on the lawn, looking straight at us like we'd come to his house. His T-shirt was tight in the shoulders, and gray with dirt.

"Who are you?" he shouted, though we were close enough.

"This is our daughter, Gina, and her good friend," Betty said. "Like we told you."

Gordon said, "Run home, Roy."

"I don't want to run home!" he shouted. "I want to stay for dinner!"

Gordon said, "You better ask your folks."

"*They* won't care."

I thought maybe he talked that loud because nobody listened to him.

I said, "Hi, Roy."

He said, "Hi, you." He had a bat in his hands, flopping it around.

Gina said, "Where'd you get that?"

Roy pointed toward the shed, stopped, shrugged and said, "This is *my* bat."

Gina looked at her dad, but he just kind of shrugged with his eyebrows. He said, "It's fine, Gina. Nobody's used that bat in years."

We went in and left Roy in the yard. Things looked the same. Pictures of Mormon temples on the walls. A hand-painted sign, done up with curlicues: FAMILIES ARE FOREVER! Which sounded like a threat. Above the dining room table there was a painting of a man with a long white beard, hands folded in prayer, sitting before a loaf of bread.

The table was set, and Betty was transferring food from pots and pans into serving dishes. Gordon rolled his shirt up past his elbows and washed at the sink like a doctor. A thwacking came from the front yard. Roy had the bat and was hitting rocks.

Gordon stuck his head out and told him to stop. Roy answered, loud enough for everyone to hear, "OK, but when are we gonna *eat?*"

Jesus, what a meal! We were supposed to be on the low-carb diet, but I took a furlough. I had a heap of mashed potatoes and two dinner rolls, and several slices of beef. Gravy! Four green beans, to be polite. I was back at those potatoes shortly. I ate myself sleepy. When things got quiet, Roy would speak up.

"My brother's coming home from his mission next month," Roy said. "He's in Korea!"

You could smell him under the food smells — sour boy. Betty said, "Shush, now, you don't have to talk so loud," and Roy said, "OK!" and rammed a fork load of potatoes into his mouth. A white clod escaped while he chewed. He picked it up and put it back. Betty had made him wash for dinner, and his hands and face seemed scalded and pink.

Gina was telling her parents how great things were for us. She told them I loved my job at the *Jackson Hole Guide*, taking photos, and that she loved hers, doing marketing at the ski hill. She didn't get into salaries or rents or broken-down cars or the looming possibility of debtor's prison.

I had a big splash of berry cobbler. I was scraping my fork edge against my plate when I noticed Gina looking at me, maybe the first time I'd felt her eyes in a week.

I smiled at her. She leaned over and put up her hand to whisper into my ear.

"You are eating like a goddamned hog."

I loved her right then, even so. I thought, *Someday this will make a great dinner-party anecdote.* She was the smartest person I knew, nasty in the rack, too good for me on several fronts. We'd moved in together three years back, and she was still the one who made me pay attention in any crowd, the one whose eyes I wanted on me, approving.

That's why I lied to her so much. Out of love.

Gordon told Roy to go home.

"I want to stay the night," Roy said, but Gordon guided him out and we all walked to the lawn and watched him ride his bike down the gravel lane. I picked up the wooden bat from the lawn. It was pocked all over by stones.

The night was coming on, cool and purple with a rim of orange on the horizon. I usually found it hard to see any beauty there on the sagebrush desert — especially compared to Jackson and the way it pushed in on you, all soaring peaks and calendar views. But in the last moments before the darkness took over, something in the sweet air and the sound of the insects made me wish I had my tripod set up and could just aim the camera and open it up for a minute or so — just paint the colors onto film.

Gordon and I talked while Betty and Gina sat in lawn chairs several feet away. He told me he'd hired men to run the place since his hip surgery; I told him about my assignments at the *Guide,* shooting criminal trials and kayak competitions. He picked at the weeds that rose at the edge of the yard, wrapping one stalk repeatedly around a thick knuckle. I wondered whether I could just write him a letter about the money and leave it behind when we left. I doubted he cared all that much, but Gina had said I'd humiliated her, and that she never wanted to be in debt to her parents again.

Still, my plan was to ask for more. Buy those ski passes, make that not a lie, and use the rest to climb out of the hole. Bury all the secrets.

We went in and sat around the living room and tried to keep up the conversation. Betty talked about an old friend of Gina's who'd told her husband she didn't want to have children. Betty said this like the woman had gone out and gotten cancer on purpose. Gordon shook his head sadly.

Gina said, "Maybe they ought to just take away her uterus altogether."

Betty got a weary look then, but no one said anything, and finally Gordon got up and turned on the TV, and we watched the local news: woman injured in car accident; ag conference at the community college; cow injured in car accident.

Then we went to bed. The first few times we visited together, they had us stay in separate rooms. Then I guess they realized there was no point in pretending we weren't good and shacked up, and they let us stay together. Neither of them had ever said a word to me about marriage. They tried to include us as a couple with Gina's married brothers and their huge broods of children — and all the silence only confirmed how much it mattered to them.

That night as we lay side by side in Gina's old bed, she said, "You have to tell him. All by yourself."

"I don't think he's going to care all that much," I said.

I took my finger and traced the outline of her ear. For a few seconds, she let me. Then she knocked my hand away.

"He'll probably like it," she said. "Big helper man. The generous patriarch."

"Well, he is helping us."

"At this point," she said, "I'd say he's helping you."

I woke up alone the next morning to the sound of Roy at the bat. I went downstairs. The house was deserted. It was nine thirty, way past breakfast. I figured I probably shouldn't go back to bed. I wished we'd smuggled in some coffee.

Betty came in the back door, wiping her hands. She'd been working in the yard, face flushed, breathing hard.

"Morning, sleepyhead," she said cheerfully.

She told me Gina had driven into town to get a few things, and Gordon was out working. "Or hollering at the workers, more like," she said.

Gordon drove out almost every day, watching over planting and harvest and butting in to show his hired men the best way. Gina said he did that because he was cheap and racist, and didn't trust the migrants he hired. She might have been right, but I thought she always made his horns out to be a little bigger than they really were. He wasn't such an asshole, and it was his place. But Gina wouldn't hear it — nothing could soften her on her parents or her hometown. Once, when I told her how friendly people were there, she said, "Give it another day or two. Keep an ear out for the fag jokes."

I walked outside, where Roy was spinning around with his arms held out, looking straight up to the sky.

"Hi, Roy," I said.

"Hi, you!" he said.

"My name's Brad."

He didn't answer. He fell woozily to the ground.

"That's really hard!" he said. "Are you married to their daughter?"

"Sort of."

"My dad says marrying my mom was the worst mistake he ever made in his life."

Gordon's truck came down the drive, and he climbed out.

"Roy," he said sharply. "Your parents must think you've moved in here."

Roy picked up a rock, tossed it and swung. The rock cracked off into the field. Gordon walked over, all lord-of-the-manor, took Roy by the neck, grabbed the bat, and said, "Go home now, son."

Roy twisted free and ran down the lane. He stopped several yards down the road, turned and said, "See you later, Brad!" and ran off again.

I watched him, wishing I could run along, too.

"What's the deal with him?" I asked.

"His folks live about a mile over." Gordon pointed across the flat land to a place I couldn't see. "They're kinda . . . rough."

"Poor?"

"No. Yes. But that's not it exactly."

"He's over here a lot?"

Gordon laughed in a way that seemed less than generous. "He's over here a lot," he said.

I asked Gordon if I could talk to him for a few minutes before lunch. As we walked toward the office he had off the garage, I thought how much more substantial he was than me in every way — thicker through the chest, stronger in the hands, firmer in the jaw, fatter in the wallet. In every basic measure.

Inside, I told him I couldn't pay him back before he sat down. Jesus, that was hard. I hadn't really disappointed him much, yet.

"Why, that's nothing to worry about," he said, like he hadn't expected it anyway. "You get it to me when you can."

A bookshelf sat behind him: *Mormon Doctrine, Lives of the Saints, Parley P. Pratt: God's Right Hand Man.* Light came through the blinds and blazed on his glasses.

"Honestly," I said, "I've run into a little more trouble."

And nothing in his face tightened up, his smile didn't drop, which made me like him a lot right then. I stammered around until he offered to help and took out his big checkbook. He wrote it for $500, like he was at peace with it.

"Here you go," he said, handing me the check like he was passing the salt. Behind him on the shelf were photographs of families, weddings, children with their hair combed neatly. Sitting there so far from all my problems, holding that crisp piece of salvation, it felt like the start of a whole new life.

"You know," I said. "We're getting married."

Gordon alerted like a bird dog. He sprinted around the desk, shook my hand and whapped me on the shoulder.

"That's great, that's great, that's just great," he kept saying. He seemed crazed, like it was better than anything he ever expected.

"It's kind of on the QT," I said.

Gina wasn't back from town so we had lunch without her. Betty sliced bread from a homemade loaf, and we toasted it at the table to go with the soup. Gordon ate six pieces, spread thick with butter. I matched him slice for slice. Before he left to go back out to the fields, he smiled at me so warmly I must have blushed, and he shook my hand, like he was welcoming me in.

I offered to help Betty in the yard. I weeded the squash and corn. I mowed the lawn and trimmed along the front step and the edge of the gravel drive. Gina came back while I was wrapping up the cord, and she gave me a long look.

Betty said, "Brad's been helping me catch up around here."

Gina said to me, with a smile that was not wholly angry, "Save some of that energy for back home."

I wheeled lava rock out to a landscaping island Betty was building in the yard, and we lay the stone around the three young trees, the bushes and the pea gravel. I took tools from her hands before she could begin a task and did it for her. When she needed a glass of water, I retrieved it.

With ice cubes. Roy was running around the edges of our work — sometimes we'd send him to the shed for a tool or let him lift a rock or two.

"Neat!" he said, watching me rake out the gravel. Betty set the sprinkler nearby.

"My dad says watering a lawn's a waste of money," Roy said.

"Your dad's right," Betty said.

Roy took off in a sprint around the house. Betty looked at me, shook her head and laughed. Her laugh was generous, though, and something about it made me want to change myself entirely — to scour my bones of sarcasm and bullshit and find some inner me who could just enjoy watching a rambunctious kid, plant trees, feel the sun. Ground under my feet. A whole lot of corny crap.

Roy ran past again, heading off on another loop around the house. Betty smiled at me, a smudge of earth on her forehead.

"Makes me think about having one of my own," I said.

She looked at me with widened eyes, but didn't say anything. Gina had her trained to stay out of our business.

"Or even a whole bunch of them," I said. "I've always loved kids."

I wasn't sure how much this contradicted anything Betty might know. Roy sprinted up to us.

"You want to see something?" he asked.

He was asking me, and I said sure, and he said we had to go out to the canal. I walked with Roy down the drive and cut across a field. He didn't say anything, just kicked at the ground and sometimes stopped to pick up rocks and throw them. He seemed like he came from a different time. I felt pleasantly removed from my life. I grew up in Chicago, and never walked down dirt lanes or skipped rocks or found things to see at the canal. We didn't pray before meals or thank God for anything. We didn't thank anyone for anything.

When we got there, Roy said, "See?" and pointed to a dead cow lodged against the bank. It was black and white, roundly swollen, legs stuck in different directions. The air smelled tart and mulchy.

"It's a dead cow!" Roy shouted.

I asked, "Are you sure?" just to play with him, and he gave me a look of disgust.

He threw a rock and hit the cow's stomach. It thumped like a drum.

"You don't know anything!"

I thought, *Exactly right, Roy. I know what the falling man knows. Look at that gravity go.* I thought about how I would ask Gina to marry me. Roy threw another rock at the cow and missed. I imagined the cow exploding, blasting its rotting mess over both of us. Maybe Roy's parents would give him a bath then.

"My dad says cows are about the stupidest fuckers on the planet!" Roy said, and it made me laugh out loud.

Then he asked if he could come to dinner again. I told him it wasn't up to me. He scuffed around some more, and suddenly ran off down the ditch bank, yelling that he'd see me later.

As he got smaller and smaller, I did the closest thing I ever did to praying, which was wishing. I wished that Roy's parents would be good to him, that they would clean him up and watch over him.

I walked back to the house. Gina and Gordon were sitting in lawn chairs out front, drinking lemonade. I went in and helped Betty get dinner ready.

After dinner came the ritual: Betty dragged out the family albums and forced Gina to look through them, while Gordon sat with his feet up in the recliner and told me stories about the multitude of branches on the family tree. All over the West, this thing spread, and they could follow it backward, back, back, back to Utah, to Illinois, to Palmyra, to England. Back to the protozoa, probably.

Betty was telling Gina a story about her great-great-whatever-grandmother. A teenage bride in Utah, witness to some buggy miracle. Go back far enough, and her family was lousy with polygamists.

"Yeah, yeah," Gina said. "The sister-wife. Gross."

Betty closed the album and set it carefully on the sofa next to her. Gina picked at a thread on her jeans. After a silence, Betty said her feet ached, and I offered to rub them. Genius improvisation, if I say so. Her feet were awful — calloused and yellow, with pointy toes and bunions. I held them in my lap, one by one, and rubbed them with the attention of a potter. I ran my thumb along the arches. I gave each toe its due. I felt really hard for the family love buried in those awful feet, and I looked at Gina every twenty seconds or so to make sure she was watching, and she was.

That night, I turned to her in bed and said, "You know what, honey? Maybe we should get married." Like I'd been swamped by a wild tide of love. And then I said, just like I'd planned, "No, wait, let me do this right."

Gina watched, waiting for the punch line. I went to her side, dropped to a knee, reached out and took her hand. It felt light as balsa, delicately hollow.

"Gina Marie Pope," I said, "may I have your father's daughter's hand in marriage?"

Her face radiated amazement or alarm.

"And that way I'll be your old man, and you'll be my old lady, officially, in the eyes of the state of Wyoming and the US of A."

She smiled. She wasn't saying no.

And then I fucked everything up. "We could tell your family," I said.

Her face closed like a flower at night.

"No way. Jesus, no. They'd freak out with happiness. Gross."

I pleaded.

"No-ho-ho," she said. "They'd be naming the grandkids in fourteen seconds."

I climbed back into bed. She said, "But you're sweet," and kissed me on the cheek. I could smell her, the way she always smelled at bedtime, like cream and flowers, and so I rolled her way. She didn't knock my hands away. Soon enough, I felt her warm palm flat against my shoulder blade.

"You're still a bastard," she whispered wetly, and bit me on the earlobe.

"A total bastard," I said, and slid on top of her.

Her mouth tasted of mint. We found a rhythm that reminded me of something deeper or better about us. She bit my nipple. It used to suck to have to be quiet so your parents wouldn't hear you, but this was fun, going easy on the bedsprings, moving so slow it could kill you. People ought to visit their parents just for that. I mean, things were fucked up. No question. My problems were circling the airport, waiting for their turn to land. But while we were there together, I had the comforting and entirely incorrect feeling that I'd done a good thing.

The next day Gina went with her parents to Twin Falls to visit some cousins, and I stayed behind and imagined all the ways that Gordon might stumble into my lie.

I took my camera and stalked the house from the gravel lane, trying to get it into the frame the way I saw it when we first drove up, three years ago. Something about the simplicity of it, the plainness. The flag pole, the green lawn, the white house, the rippling surface of the barley. Now it was a place I knew.

Roy rode up the lane on his bike. He slammed the brakes and skidded, raising a small cloud of dust.

He asked what I was doing, and when I told him I was

trying to take pictures of the house, he asked why, and I told him I didn't know. He asked if my camera cost a lot of money, and I said yeah, probably.

He was definitely wearing the same clothes this time. I was sure. He seemed visibly dirtier, more hyperactive. Ignored. I thought I should do something, and I felt pressed by the fact that I would most likely do nothing. Couldn't I be someone else, for once?

I said, "Let's go look at the cow."

We walked down the canal bank. Roy kept running ahead of me and jumping, landing sideways in a kind of slide. And then he'd yell, "He's safe!" or "He's under the tag!" At the cow, Roy threw two rocks and they drummed off the bulging belly, which seemed to be expanding even as we watched. He turned to me and smiled. His teeth were yellow and scungy.

"Why don't you take me to your place?" I asked.

I didn't know what I wanted, exactly. I wanted to set someone straight, kick someone's ass, brush someone's teeth. Roy shrugged and watched the ground.

"Come on," I said. "Let's go."

I took him by the arm.

"Come on," I repeated. "Then we'll go bat some rocks."

He got on his bike and started riding slowly enough for me to walk beside him. We went down the canal bank, until he turned onto a dirt road between two fields and headed toward a house and clump of trees.

Roy didn't say anything while we went. His house was

white gone gray, with veiny, cracking paint. A lawnmower sat on the porch. The front door was wide open, a dark gap in the house's surface. When we got to the edge of the yard, Roy stopped.

"Come on," I said.

He sat down and wrapped his arms around his knees.

Right then I knew there was something awful in that house. I don't believe in that stuff, intuition, but I *knew* that when I walked into that house I was going to find a body or a note or something I couldn't imagine. My breath was coming faster than I could get it out. I walked up the stairs and across the threshold into the shadowy room and waited in fear for my eyes to adjust.

A woman came into the front room wiping her hands on a dish towel. She was pretty, brown hair pulled back, plain and capable looking. She seemed a little alarmed to find a stranger in her living room—a room that, now that I noticed, seemed only ordinary, no bodies or notes, nothing fancy or horrifying.

"Can I help you?" she asked.

"I'm sorry," I said. "I didn't know anyone was home."

"So you came in?"

"I'm with Roy."

She stayed back from me, but didn't seem scared. I couldn't think how to explain myself.

"Roy?" she asked, looking around me. I thought for a second that she didn't know Roy—that he had taken me to someone else's house, had played a joke, told a lie. But then

I realized that she was just asking where he was. I backed into the doorway, and looked out at him, still squatted in the yard, and called his name.

This whole time, the woman stayed where she was. When Roy came in, she said, "What have you been doing, son?"

He said, "Playing with Brad. Throwing rocks at the cow."

"Throwing rocks at the cow," she said, looking at me. "Roy, go clean yourself up."

"Let me explain," I said. "I'm married to Gordon and Betty's daughter."

Like that, her face opened up.

"Gina?" she asked. "I didn't know she'd gotten married."

"Yes, ma'am," I said. "I'm Brad. Brad Knight."

She invited me to sit down and offered me a glass of lemonade. The living room was worn and plain, but clean. Some of the same Mormon stuff on the walls that Gina's folks had — a photo of a temple, the painting of the bearded man praying over bread. Roy came out, and he looked clean now, hair wet and lined with the teeth of a comb.

He didn't need any help from me.

She asked me some questions about myself. I think I caught her looking at my ringless finger. For some reason, I wanted to shake her by the shoulders. I wanted to squeeze her bones. I was sick with adrenaline. Every problem in my life gathered outside the bunker, ready to lob in grenades.

"I work for *National Geographic*," I said. "Shooting photos."

She probably didn't realize just what a lottery winner of life that would have made me.

"Travel all over on assignment. I was in Nepal last month, shooting the Dalai Lama. Next week I'm off to the Sudan."

"I've seen his camera!" Roy said.

"That sounds exciting," she said.

"It's OK," I said. "Gina's in finance. *Arbitrage.* She's an *arbitrageur.*" I tried to say it Frenchly.

"Do you have any children?"

"Yes. Yes, we do. We have four children. Two boys and two girls."

Her face betrayed a little confusion.

I said, "Let's see. There's Sheila, she's the oldest. She's thirteen and starting to discover boys." I rolled my eyes in mock exasperation. "Bobby's eleven. Loves the soccer. Frank is seven and he's our little nerd. Likes to read about dinosaurs and do math. And Sheila, she's the youngest. She's the little baby."

"Her name's Sheila, too?"

I wanted to say: Of fucking course her name's not Sheila, and yet if I told you right now that it was, said, *Yes, we named both of our daughters Sheila,* we'd just make that the truth, you and I.

"Did I say Sheila?" I asked, chuckling. "I always do that. Shelly."

She looked like she was working math problems in her head.

"You mean Gina Pope, right?"

"Yes, ma'am."

"She's got a thirteen-year-old daughter?"

It occurred to me that this woman probably knew when Gina graduated from high school or something.

"Honestly, we're hoping that Sheila gets a little bun in the oven in the next couple of years. A lot of people think it's too soon for that, but Gina and me, we want to be grandparents before we're 35. Look, it's not so unusual. Most societies get the girls into breeding at a very young age, in their teens. I mean, the plumbing's all there. Why not get things rolling?"

"Well, that seems . . ."

"Maybe she and Roy?"

I let the question hang in the air. She cleared her throat. Roy wore a look of confusion.

"I should probably let you get back," she said, standing and reaching for my empty glass.

I felt a whoosh of air inside.

"You know," I said. "Roy's running around kind of wild."

She stopped, holding an empty glass in each hand, pinpricks of color appearing in her cheeks.

"What do you mean?"

"Unsupervised, in the dirt and fields, poking around at dead animals. Wearing the same clothes every day."

"I guess you should mind your own business," she said, so quietly I almost didn't hear it. "Leave now."

Her eyes had grown wet. I thought she might get mad

and throw a glass or something, but she was collapsing. Roy picked at the carpet.

I stood and walked to the door like someone whose purpose and meaning are simply laid out before him, a dotted line to follow all of his days. I turned in the doorway and said, "I'm serious. I'll take Roy myself and we'll raise him in our home, have him get my daughter knocked up, whatever, sure — just fill the house with babies, and we'll take care of them all, keep them clean and safe, and keep them all away from people like you."

I was almost out of their yard when I heard Roy yell my name. I turned around. He was standing in the open doorway.

"You're an asshole," he said.

I thought, *Exactly right, Roy. The falling man never gains speed, though it seems that he should.* I lifted a hand goodbye.

Walking back, I thought of all the ways this might come back against me. I didn't mind. Maybe Gina could even find it funny, if I told it right. The sun was low in the sky as I walked through the fields and along the canal bank. The cow cast a round shadow on the water.

Gina was waiting in the yard at her parents' house.

"Did you tell my dad we were getting married?" she asked.

"I guess so."

She looked at me closely, like she wanted to see whatever it was about me that she'd never guessed at.

I said, "I just wanted to make him happy for some reason. I thought you might say yes. How the fuck do I know?"

Then she smiled. "Well, he's good and pissed off now," she said.

I was pretty wiped out, after all that, which is the only excuse I can make. We were sitting in the living room after dinner, our last night there, and Betty was doing her best to calm us all with the dull details of my life.

"Where did you go to college again, Brad?"

"Tuscaloosa. University of Alabama. Graduated in 1993."

I was half asleep, and it popped out. Stated like an incontrovertible fact. Gina looked at me incredulously. "You did not," she said.

I froze. I looked at her and somehow couldn't retrieve whatever it was that I needed from my mind to patch this over. Here's the thing: I used to say I graduated from the University of Alabama, but that was not what I said anymore. What I said now was that I spent two years at a community college in Big Bend, and then graduated from the University of New Mexico. In 1994. There was a lesson in this, somewhere. I couldn't figure out how to bridge my way back.

Gina looked at me steadily. Finally, I shook my head and said, "I don't know what's wrong with me. I'm so sleepy."

Gina said, "So sleepy that you thought you graduated from the University of Alabama in 1993?"

I laughed.

She watched me for several more seconds, and when she finally broke the gaze, I looked at her father. I saw that he knew all he needed to know about me — that I was false in my bones. Then everybody just started talking again. I tucked inside, into my mind, and meticulously went through everything — everything I said about my parents, everything I said about my high school days, everything I said about my old girlfriends, what sports I played in high school, the family religion, every little surface of life. I tried to tell myself that it was all intact, and that no one had seen in.

Driving back to Jackson, I felt like I'd been somewhere farther away. Gina was quiet. It felt like the bad times might be mostly over. That round, anyway.

We drove through Idaho Falls and Island Park and Henry's Fork and West Yellowstone. We wound through the park, and we didn't stop at anything, just watched out the windows as we passed bison and bubbling mud and the open valleys. We got stuck in a line for roadwork. I asked Gina if she wanted to think up any new ways to kill me.

"No," she said. "I thought of them all."

"Good."

"I'm prepared."

"Good."

After a silence, she said, "Maybe we can get married."

"Really?" I said.

"I don't know," she said. "Maybe."

There are times when your groove and the groove of all things just line up and become the same groove. Nothing that happens has to be real, and anything is possible. This was that. We didn't say much as we drove the rest of the way home.

Pocket Dog

THIS STARTS IN THE hot pool, around my fourth vodka cran, when she comes in slapping the poolside with her flip-flops, looking like someone you see getting out of a car on TV. Huge sunglasses with tan lenses. Pressed blond hair and bronze skin. Her thin, golden legs emerging from a denim skirt that looked expensively worn out. I believe firmly in watching such a woman. The other men in the hot pool, the ones under the supervision of their own women, were trying not to. She stepped out of that skirt and bent over, ass up like an autumn doe, a taut, aqua patch of swimsuit summoning the eye. It was four in the afternoon, and something started flopping inside me like a fish on a riverbank.

Another one came in, a little shorter and chubbier. The first girl, tall and thin, called out, "Hey, bitch," and the second one said, "Hey, bitch, I got your drink." The second one carried two plastic cups with bubbles and chunks of lime.

She held a purse in the crook of her arm, and from the purse emerged the tiny head of a creature with a furious puff of Einstein hair. Like a rat being born. The rat barked and hung a tongue the color of pencil eraser.

Out here, we're bound to feel a dog like that is just wrong. It makes us feel defensive about our whole lives.

I stood to get another drink. I felt my suit drain and grip me all over. It made me feel naked, that everyone else was naked too, practically, and the sensation I got — a sensation I often got when the number of drinks was somewhere in the middle range and there was a prospect in the water — was that we were all deliriously close to fucking. I'm nobody's motivational speaker, but if I've learned anything it's this: Always try to fuck someone you think won't fuck you. Just try. Chances are decent that you're overestimating their taste or intelligence.

One of the girls turned her head my way, but with her huge sunglasses I couldn't tell if she was looking at me or just something in my hemisphere. I visualized sliding a finger inside the high, elastic legband of her swimsuit. I wondered if she was tan all over, or if she had the pale ghost of a bikini on her skin.

I stepped out of the hot pool, just as the girls were stepping in. They made soft moaning noises as they sank. They held their drinks up and talked close to each other, laughing.

I stood dripping at the bar window until Parker showed up and asked, "Another?"

I turned and watched the girls bob in the water. They

rested their backs against the tiled barrier between the hot pool and cool pool.

"If you insist," I said.

A high roof covered the hot end, opening onto the mountains beyond. Wisps of steam curled off the water. The girls held their heads close together, and they might have been looking at me. I thought about the three of us, naked Twister, trying to keep up. For all I knew, it was shaping up as a day to remember. The rat gave a ratty bark. He was still in the purse, head out, resting on the poolside bench and nervously sniffing the chlorine air.

"Hi, Bubby," the taller girl said, and then she swim-walked over to the poolside near the dog. "Are you OK, little Bubby? Little Bubby-wubby?"

She laughed a sarcastic laugh.

Her friend said, "Shut *up*. I hate that shit. He's a *dog*."

They laughed far too hard.

"But he's so cute," said the tall one, moving smoothly through the water, just her head, shoulders and drink exposed. "He's just a little darling."

"Fuck. You," the second one said, and they both laughed as though they couldn't catch their breath. "That little darling would shit in your hair."

Parker handed me my drink through the sliding glass window.

"You should make some new friends," he said, nodding toward them.

"My thoughts exactly," I said. "You know them?"

"Nope. But they seem like your type."

"Which is what?"

"Decrepit. Intoxicated. Kind of hot."

"Sounds right."

"A little stupid. You should give them your Montana land-baron shtick."

"It's no shtick, my friend."

Parker leaned on his forearms in the bar window and watched the girls closely.

I walked back to the pool and heard him slide the bar window closed. I used to think that kind of banter was fun. Now, there were days I could hardly stand to talk to him. Days that I thought maybe I should just get a case of something and hole up in my room.

This wasn't one of those days. It seemed like something all right might happen. Something additional. Like I wouldn't be the only one asking him for one more drink, just one more, after last call.

Grandma said the problem around here started with the death of work. The place just doesn't run on work any more — it runs on leisure, on fly fishing and mountain biking and skiing. People moving in with their money already made. The rail yard closed a couple years back, and some doomsday cult was building bunkers down by Yellowstone, and ranchers were subdividing and selling. The lines of the pioneers — Grandma liked to think of us all that way, as pioneer stock — were weakening and leaving the land.

I agreed with her, though I've always done as little as possible myself.

"These people don't have anything better to do than look for someplace to spend a hundred dollars on dinner," she said.

That was one of her grand examples of the world gone stupid: hundred-dollar dinners. Others were: catch-and-release fishing, Michael Dukakis, dogs named after mountain ranges, precious horse people.

"Can a whole economy survive just on spending?" she would ask. "You tell me. You went to college."

"I studied land management."

"Maybe you should manage some land."

When I came out here, the idea was that I'd run the place. Grandma told me it was my parents' idea, but that was just a little horseshit to make me feel better. She told me it was a last-chance kind of deal, but I knew I'd already run out of final chances with my parents, and they wouldn't want me attached to the ranch once Grandma was gone. Lucky for them, I never came close to managing the place. She had Lanny, her man, and Lanny knew what he was doing.

He took me out one day shortly after I got here, drove me to the eastern fence line at the foot of the Absarokas. He barely spoke as we bumped across the field, the smell of hot dust and plastic inside the truck. Lanny wore a pair of leather gloves gone gray brown, the same shade as his low-heeled work boots. At the fence, barbed wire hung slack between the leaning posts. We got out and he said, "You get that wire puller, and I'll spool on the new wire." He lifted the blocky spool onto one shoulder and grabbed a pair of wire cutters. I looked into the back of the truck — over the machine parts and tools and coils of rope — and couldn't guess which object was a wire puller. He wound up doing everything that day. He never even pretended I was in charge.

Grandma and I used to like sitting on her big front porch, in the Adirondack chairs she bought in Oregon. She liked to tell the story of the shop on the coast where she found the chairs, of the man in the straggly beard and skin weathered like a beach shack. Everything in the whole goddamned place had a story. The salt and pepper shakers. The wine glasses. I guess she didn't find it sad, defining the objects of her life by their location in the past, but it was one of the things that eventually drove me out, put me on a temporary vacation. Just then I wanted to be living a new life.

Sometimes on the porch, we'd watch a sunset together, the sky shining in pink and purple and gold, the light sliding along the Crazies and the Gallatins, wrinkling the mountainsides in shadow. It really was the most beautiful thing, the kind of thing you can't really talk about because nobody wants to hear anything simple and nice, not even Grandma.

"It makes you sick to think about," she said once after a long silence. "Hundred-dollar dinners. My father never made a hundred dollars in a year."

"He owned this."

"Yeah, but land wasn't crazy then. Everybody had some. That didn't mean they stopped working."

She meant me, but she wasn't too harsh about it. She was a nice woman, at bottom, and for close to a year she had not tried to stop me from doing the things I did. I probably loved her more than anybody. Some mornings I'd come in with the sun, and she'd be up for breakfast, and we'd sit down together, and I'd try real hard not to slur my words or pass out in my eggs, and she never said a word, just acted like we were both starting off our days, our regular everyday lives. Then I'd go and sleep until dinner.

We made friends, me and the girls with the rat dog. I settled back into the pool with my drink and watched them with a little smile, let them know I was watching, and pretty soon we were talking. I should make something clear: I am no one's idea of good-looking. Most of my hair is gone on top, and I don't bother all that much about grooming the fringes. I've got a belly like Buddha, with some bare remnant of an athlete underneath. But I'm tall, and that seems to matter, at least in the bar light. And I'm up for fun, have some leisure time and money. I try to listen to what the ladies have to say, and don't generally get caught watching somebody better-looking coming through the door. I tell outrageous stories. I'm up for taking the party to its natural limit, not too bothered by the untimely arrival of sunrise. I believe the ugliest man in America could get laid daily if he had a little money and gumption.

Anyway, these girls were the dirtiest talkers I'd ever heard in my life. They called each other gash and felch queen. They talked about the guys they'd had sex with, laughed about their pinky cocks. For me, this was an entirely unsuspected world. For me, hot, nasty girls were a pornographic fiction. Women just didn't talk this way, not the ones I knew — not even the ones that you could shake free of their panties in the parking lot of a bar. Even those women, in my experience, required the standard kinds of fakery, the whispery bullshit.

These girls, though — I kind of loved it.

I hadn't thought I could still be scandalized.

Somehow, we got to talking about anal sex. I said the other varieties hadn't bored me yet.

Short said, "I'm saving it for my husband."

"You liar," said Tall. "Austin said he popped you in the bathroom at Pure."

Short screeched in fake outrage.

"He told you that? He did?"

Tall laughed and laughed.

"I did *not*," Short said. "Suck my balls."

"I would so suck your balls."

They laughed hysterically.

Later, we sat poolside and looked at people through our sunglasses as the night fell down. Tall picked up a copy of the *Bozeman Daily Chronicle*. I noticed the date — August 23, 1988 — and realized I hadn't considered the day or date or year in what felt like forever. She opened the paper wide in front of her face. Short, sitting to her right, leaned over, unscrewed the top of a small, smoky gray vial and removed a tiny spoon. She held the spoon to each of Tall's nostrils, and the sound of snorting vanished behind the splashing from the pool.

"You should really read this article, Simon," Tall said to me.

"You bet," I said. "Hand it over."

These girls were really something. I thought I might be in love with one of them. Either one. I thought I might have lived my whole life preparing to exist only in relation to them, swimming in perpetual intoxication.

The hot springs had a hotel and six cabins, the pools, and a restaurant that was always getting written up in the *New York Times*. The food was fantastic — demi-glace this, cream-reduction that, Ted Turner's grass-fed bison. I had taken Cabin No. 6, at the end of the row. Every day someone came in and cleaned it, made the bed, left clean towels. When I came back, it was like I'd never been.

I had a suitcase filled with my own special pharmacy. Mostly downers. Druggy drugs. A sticky lump of weed big as your fist. A bunch of cocaine bindles. A baggie full of pills I couldn't keep straight. There for a while it was kind of fun taking one and then waiting to find out what would happen.

I came here after Grandma started asking What I Was Going To Do With My Life. Out of everyone I knew, she was the last to ask. God love her, but it seemed unnecessary.

"You can't live off me forever," she said.

I didn't ask why not, which is the problem with that whole

kind of discussion. You can't just say something simple and true.

"What are you about, Simon? That's what I want to know. What is your life going to be about?"

What I was about was pretty apparent. It didn't require a lot of description. We were on the porch right then, late afternoon filling up the valley with light, and I was having the day's first cup of coffee. Grandma was looking at me like a prosecuting attorney. With her dusty black hair and small, wiry frame, she reminded me of a walnut, parched and intricate.

"All this talk about purpose," I said, avoiding her stare. Then I couldn't think of what else to add, and she let it go.

I figured my parents had gotten to her. I thought: *I'm not hurting anybody. Who says you have to live a sad-sack life full of Mondays?*

So I took a little break and went to the hot springs. It's not like I was hiding or anything. We'd been going there forever. Grandma always told how her father lent the money to have the springs developed. It was the first place anyone would have looked for me then, besides jail.

After closing, me and Parker and the girls sat in the hot pool. The girls were from Boise, of all places. One of their fathers started a microchip company back in the early '80s and sold it. The other one's dad patented something for Hewlett-Packard. The girls said they were on vacation for they didn't know how long.

Parker asked them, "Are you in school?"

Short said, "Not anymore. How old do you think we are?"

Parker guessed twenty-two; I guessed twenty-four.

"We are not," they said to both guesses, but they never really answered, they just laughed and laughed.

Later, after Tall and I had decamped to my room, she was sitting on my lap resting her head on my shoulder. I was feeling buried under all the drinks and coke and pills, but I thought I could perform. I wanted to sleep, but I wasn't sure I could. Her skin felt like a child's skin, like skin that hadn't begun to deteriorate. She smelled like cigarettes and perfume. Her breath was bad, but not very. I ran a hand down her arm and onto her hip.

"Hey," she said a little sloppily into my ear. "I'm not doing anything sexual with you."

And she snuggled closer.

When I first moved in with Grandma, about six years after college and about six weeks after Mom and Dad finally cut me off, she sat me down and explained her vision for how the ranch should be run.

There were still cattle, though not many. She felt cattle weren't the future. She'd started letting fishing guides pay to bring clients out to fish the spring creeks. She'd even talked about putting in some cabins or a little raw-log motel at the far end of the property, out of sight from the house, but my parents didn't want her to do that, and the land would be theirs soon. Grandma said tourism was the only way to go.

A campground, cabins, arrangements with guides — something. "You'll eventually have no choice," she said.

But she wanted me to wait until she was gone. She wanted me to promise her that. This was when she was still pretending that my promises might have a bearing on the ranch itself. Before the day I went out with Lanny to mend fence. Though I'd spent summers at the ranch throughout my childhood, and though I could ride and rope in a pinch, I was a soft, self-indulgent boy. I was then, and I am now. It's OK with me. I dislike laziness in others a lot more than in myself. Dad used to give me these speeches all the time, the nobility of labor, etc. I've had girlfriends who took a similar tack.

One day shortly after I'd arrived, I was sitting with a whiskey on the front porch. An April afternoon. It was just getting pretty during the days, still cold at night. From the porch, everything looked green and firm, but it was muddy in the fields, and Lanny came in to use the phone when he got his pickup stuck. I had my feet up and sunglasses on, an unread book in my lap. I watched him as he stood at the bottom of the stairs, lifted his muddy right boot and pulled it off, stepped onto the bottom step and then did the same with his left one. I thought what a practical man he was, and how I would have trailed mud onto the steps and the porch and right on into the house.

When Lanny squinted at me, I could tell that I presented an unbelievable picture to him: drinking in the middle of the day, feet up, a grown man on his ass with a book.

He went in and made a call. When he came back and sat on the steps, pulling the boots on, neither of us said anything for a couple of minutes. I was trying to figure out how to stay out of the mud without appearing to want to stay out of the mud. I believe this is one of the keys to life.

Finally, I said, "Think you've got it handled out there?"

Lanny looked at me and smiled, putting on a friendly face. Wherever I am for the rest of my life, I will think of him at that moment as the perfectly formed human adult.

"I think we'll manage," he said.

I woke to a knock on the door. Sometime during the night, I had moved over to my bed. Tall was sleeping, curled in the chair. After all that glorious, nasty talk, it was a disappointing way to wake up, both of us still in our underwear.

"Let me in, Simon," my grandmother's voice said, and I thought maybe I was hallucinating. It was one thirty in the afternoon, and I wanted very badly to go back to sleep. I put my feet on the floor and waited for the rolling to stop. I slipped into the white robe hanging in the closet and opened the door.

Grandma stood on the cabin's little front step. She was wearing jeans and a snap-button shirt with faded paisley patterns.

"Simon, we're here to talk to you," she said.

The sunlight hurt my eyes. "We?" I asked.

"Lanny and I," she said.

He was sitting in the driver's seat of his big work truck. I could just make out his shape inside the shady cab. I lifted a hand in greeting.

"I'm kind of in the middle of something," I said.

"Simon, it's long past time for a talk," she said again.

Her words and her manner conveyed the sense that she had rehearsed this. She seemed nervous, which was strange because she never seemed nervous.

"This bullshit will not stand, Simon," she said, all forceful. "We need you to come with us."

I realized then what this was about, and the disappointment that swelled under me was so large and fast moving that I was washed in vertigo. My intervention. This was my intervention. Fourteen years of true debauchery, a heroic effort, and all the forces of propriety could muster were Grandma and Lanny. I had always imagined something a little grander — a crowd, some heartfelt tears, a security guard or two standing by with restraints. Every drunk loves a little weepy-huggy. I thought, *You should find this funny. Why don't you find this fucking hilarious?* An ache flashed through my ribs.

I shut the door in Grandma's face.

The tall girl sat up in the chair, bleary faced and no longer attractive. I wondered which one of us was making the room smell that way, and then I realized it was the dog. I didn't remember the dog, but there he was, sitting on the other chair, rubbery tongue and beady eyes, proud of the fingerling turds he'd left around the room.

"What's going on?" the girl asked.

"We've been surrounded," I said, putting the chain on the door. I couldn't remember her name.

I started pulling the curtains and blinds.

Grandma knocked and shouted my name.

I catalogued possible ways out of the cabin, and none of them were suited. There was no back door. Two windows were big enough to crawl out of, but you'd have been spotted either way.

I sat down on the bed and opened my suitcase.

"This calls for a little something something," I said.

"What is this about?" the girl asked. She was in a foul mood.

"Just a little family disagreement," I said, getting out the rolling papers and weed.

We passed the bone back and forth until the cabin reeked of skunky smoke. Grandma stopped knocking. I started feeling like she was there to steal something from me. I don't mean that I didn't understand why she was there, but on some animal level, it felt like an attack on the very core of Who I Am As A Person. I believe that Who I Am As A Person is my own business, just as Who You Are As A Person is yours, and both may require defending at some point, and that particular Waterloo, my friend, could be the thing that defines your entire life.

Or something like that. I wanted to draw the cabin around me tighter.

"Simon? We're not going away. We're going to stay out here until you talk to us. We love you, Simon, but this bullshit will not stand."

Tall started giggling. "What a Nazi," she said.

"Don't talk about my grandmother," I said.

"Sorry," she said, sarcastically. "She seems nice."

"I didn't mean don't talk bad about my grandmother," I said. "I meant don't talk about my grandmother. At all."

She looked away from me, a little embarrassed, but not much. I tried a white pill with a red band around the middle. I offered her one and she took it. Her dog lifted his rat leg and fired a stream against the wall. I was getting tired of her, to be honest, so I said, "Look, are we going to fuck or are we going to sit around blabbing?" and I was right, that did it, she said, "Let me shower first," and then we did everything, with Grandma right outside, and this girl was good, she was fine, but I have to say she wasn't all that I expected, not from all that talk. She was just an ordinary disappointing person.

Eventually Lanny came to the door. The girl was packing, and I was lying on the bed. The image of him out there, competent Lanny, flooded me with shame, and so I opened the door. He stood there in his solid way, jeans low over his work boots, a denim shirt over a T-shirt, tiny glistening eyes.

"Come on, now, Simon," he said. "This is wearing your grandma out."

I could see her standing back by the truck, rubbing her face.

"I'm sorry you got dragged into this," I said.

"I'm the last person out of a whole hell of a lot of people you should be sorry for."

But he was the one there. What I felt right then was tired. Like my whole frame was melting. That was it. Tired enough to crawl into bed and sleep through winter.

"You're right," I said. "You're completely right. I see that now. I'm coming out, and we can head right over to Big Timber, if that's what you want, and I can check myself in."

He looked at me without expression. I said, "I'll be right out," and closed the door.

I took three different pills and chased them with the last inch of vodka in a bottle. The girl watched me gather clothes and stuff them into my suitcase, then said, "I've got to get out of here."

I looked up briefly. Though we'd been all tangled up in each other not an hour earlier, she looked like someone I'd never met, someone whose life I could not imagine because there was no piece of it touching mine.

"Thanks for everything," I said. She rolled her eyes and left.

I came out with my suitcases. Lanny was waiting, and Grandma had climbed into the passenger seat of the pickup. Twilight was stretching all the shadows.

"I want to thank you," I said to Lanny. "You didn't have to do this."

He squinted at me coldly, like he was assessing a sick calf.

"I work for your grandmother," he said. "That's what this is."

So I found myself riding in Lanny's truck for a second time. Grandma sat in the middle, but she wasn't talking. She was angry, and silence is how we do anger in my family. Our shoulders were touching, and our legs, and we sometimes jostled into each other when Lanny took a turn or hit a bump. The pickup smelled like manure and heater dust. The valley looked like heaven to me right then, open wide to possibility, the light aslant through the peaks, and it made me think of Lewis and Clark, of buckskin and flintlocks, all the silly bullshit we repeat here, year after year.

It was an hour's drive to Big Timber. I felt like maybe I would start to see things correctly from there on out. What I could not see was that I would enter rehab and Grandma would visit me every day and sit in a chair with her copy of *The Big Sky*. I thought that I'd get healthy and sober, but I started smoking like a fiend in rehab, two packs a day and then more, hanging my arm out the window damn near all day, looking across the wide plain toward the Crazies. I haven't had a drink since then, somehow, but I still smoke like a drunk.

In the truck, Lanny put on a staticky AM station out of Livingston. It would be dark by the time we got there. Once I got registered, got settled into the cute little bedroom cell, Grandma would visit every day for three months, which was the best part then and is the worst part now, because after

I got out and moved away, I stayed away. I finished rehab and moved to Seattle and got a job working with a salmon-preservation nonprofit and married a real woman. When Grandma had her stroke, I didn't visit. When she died, I didn't come back. I stayed away, with my new life and nothing to crowd away what I remembered of the old one. Leaving isn't something you do just once. You've got to stick with it. If I could talk to her now, I would say, *That's what I'm about, Grandma. You said you wanted to know.*

I've got about half my inheritance left.

When we were riding to Big Timber in Lanny's truck, I watched the gray night sifting in, and I went over the previous couple of days in my head. I do that still, think about those days at the hot springs and those girls with that stupid dog. The very thought of them seems ridiculous. The whole idea of their lives. I could never explain it to anyone I know now, and that makes me miss something, a certain mind-set, the framework that might allow a person to soak, drunk, in warm water, just waiting for the next thing.

I remember when we were first starting to talk, me and the girls with the pocket dog. We were drunk, but not yet ridiculous. I was telling them stories about myself, some true, some not, and they were delighting in catching the lies.

I told them I was a rodeo clown.

"You are not," Tall would say, and Short would say, sometimes at the exact same moment, "You are *not*."

I told them I was an astronaut, a llama rancher, a river guide, a land speculator, a cocaine dealer. They laughed and laughed. I felt like the funniest man on earth. I told them I was a grizzly wrestler, a former pro-football player, a hog butcher. I thought for sure that it was going to be the three of us in one bed, a story for the ages. They laughed and laughed, and I watched the water slither around their skin, shine in droplets on their tan shoulders and darken the tips of their hair, and with everything I said I drew further and further away from myself, and with everything I said they cried, over and over again, "You are not. You are *not*."

Godforsaken Idaho

FOR MOST OF MY LIFE I couldn't have found Idaho on a map. I had no picture of the place in my mind, nothing like a California beach or a Texas oil field. Potato trees, is what I thought on the drive out. Rows and rows of potato trees. I was a stupid child, well into adulthood. So I find myself in Idaho, and it turns out that potatoes grow underground, and there aren't any up here in the northern part of the state anyway. People here hate it if you even mention potatoes. I feel that way now, too.

Once I came home from work around midnight and found the landlord sitting on my front step smoking a cigarette, all jittery eyes and foul breath, his cane resting beside him.

"You know about them over there?" he asked, waving his cigarette toward the house across the street. "Witches.

Witches. It's not a joke, man. It's not a fucking joke. Don't act like it is."

He looked at me intently, trembling. He had one yellow eye and one gray. A hammock of hairy belly hung from beneath his shirt. I wanted to walk around him, but it would have been impolite.

I said, "Everybody knows witchcraft is no joke."

I'd lived there four or five months by then, and I can't say I was surprised we'd reached this point. But this was a new strata of crazy. He turned toward the neighbor's house and began yelling.

"I know you're watching me, bitches. *I know it*. And you're going to regret it. You're going to fucking regret it, because you think you've got the strong witchcraft but you haven't seen anything until you've seen my witchcraft, motherfuckers."

His face burned, magenta above his gray, bristling beard.

I said, "Look, I'm tired. I've just finished at work, and — "

"Right, right, right, right, right," he said.

He struggled to his feet, and his voice rose in pitch.

"Too tired. Too tired." He began to mimic a whine. "I'm too tired. I work hard all day, and when I come home I'm too tired to talk, too tired to do anything but go into my apartment and read my dirty magazines" — he was spitting the words and spitting actual spit, little bits of his foul-smelling breath landing on me.

He moved toward me on the sidewalk, lumbering on his unsteady legs, then stopped. He leaned into my face, breath like fish and bile, and jabbed me with the hard end of a finger.

"I want my money," he said.

He slowly climbed the stairs to his apartment.

That's what he always said to me, every time. I want my money.

My magazines. I don't like to think of them as dirty. I consider myself a collector. An aficionado. I've got them in chronological order, seven stacks of twelve across the top shelf of the closet. *Penthouse,* 1981–1985. And counting. I love the feel of the magazines themselves, heavier and slicker than a normal magazine, plumping outward from the staples. My favorite pictorials involve sleek modernist rooms, Eames chairs and square black sofas, everything cold but the flesh, and a brilliant city night somewhere outside. I hate beach scenes, girly bedrooms, faux barnyards. Show me the world's most beautiful woman with a foot propped up on a hay bale and all I can think about is that ridiculous hay bale.

The magazines have moved with me every step of my adult life. I started keeping them a few years after high school, in my Chicago apartment. I couldn't afford that place, and soon the magazines moved with me back to Mom's. And now, some years later, out here.

Mom found the magazines once, but by then she had forgotten who I was. She'd started calling me Howard — my dad's name — all the time.

"This explains so much, Howard," she said, holding the glossy pages open to a scene of two women placing the tips of their tongues together. She wore a nightdress and had one hand on her walker. "You can forget about ever touching me again."

I always thought the stroke stole my mother's personality, but maybe it just revealed it. She became a mean old lady. Her voice turned crabbed and harsh, and she would tell her aides they were stupid on a daily basis. "Moron!" she would hiss, as they sorted through a drawer stuffed with receipts she refused to throw away. I started to forget the old her, and then I stopped wanting to live there. Supposedly I was taking care of her, but her aides did everything except put fresh cans of soda in front of her. If she'd ever needed my help in the bathroom, I might have run out the door.

So that was the start of it, the trailhead to godforsaken Idaho. I took a few things and a little money and pointed my Ford Fiesta onto Interstate 90. Three days later, I rounded a freeway curve, came upon a glittering blue lake and decided to stop awhile. Or maybe the start was Dad's heart attack, five years earlier. What I remember about that is a word: infarction. Great word. It sounds like what it does to you. Infarks you. You're infarked. We lived in Lake Forest then, and we were rich before and no longer rich afterward, but we became better acquainted with vascular terminology. Dad was young for such a big attack, the doctor said, but it wasn't much of a surprise. He drank Scotch and put pats of butter on his steaks and went around hot faced all the time, just this side of an outburst. I loved him without a choice in the matter, but after he died I felt my life bloom with possibility. New vistas were springing open, I could feel it. This, it turns out, was wrong. I was still in high school then, and all I did with my new vistas was fail to enroll in college. Dad would have killed me for that, just shot me in the head before taking another big slurp of Glenfiddich. You could see those kinds of fantasies in his eyes.

The magazines. I could imagine no way my landlord would know about them unless he'd been in my apartment. Sneaking in while I was away, putting his filthy hands all over my life. I started booby-trapping the place. A hair balanced on the handle of a drawer. A bit of tape between the foot of the bathroom door and the jamb. A note inside a drawer: "Hello, asshole!" Then I'd come home and examine the traps, and I could never tell. Had that hair been moved and replaced? Had the tape simply come unstuck? Had he been in here, or was it just me?

Sometimes I left, locked the front door, drove to the neighboring cul-de-sac, parked, walked back through the weedy field between that dead end and my own, climbed the fence, and slipped in through my back window. Lights off, shades down. I'd put on my camping headlight and sit in a closet with a few magazines and a novel. I was lonely then, soaked with it, gorging on porn and the great books. Just then it was the Russians. During the closet days, I was reading *The Idiot*, pages stained with petroleum jelly.

. . .

When I first moved in, I thought I'd be nice to the landlord. I invited him for coffee. He sat at my tippy kitchen table, sideways in his chair with both hands on his cane. He told me he hoped I was better than the last tenant, who had a real problem with honesty. When he talked, he ran his tongue along his fat lower lip and left an oily sheen. He told me the bitches across the street were always watching him, and if I knew what was good for me, I'd never have anything to do with them.

He slurped his coffee. He looked around the apartment frankly.

"You should decorate this place," he said. "Hang a picture. Maybe get a plant or two."

I said, "Yeah, maybe," and then I asked him about the winters, and he talked about the winters for a long time, how the city had in it for him, and so they never plowed the cul-de-sac, the fuckers, and how all the people moving in from California didn't know how to drive in the snow. Then he said, "But seriously, guy. You've got to dress it up in here."

I thought he was just lonely and strange, which made us kin.

I never ended up getting a phone. I could no longer see any reason to talk to my mother, and everybody else was a minor character. I thought for a while that maybe I'd hear from someone through the mail—maybe Joe Tran from high school, maybe my uncle Jack—but nothing personal ever came in with the bills.

The second time I invited the landlord in, it was about

three weeks later. He huffed his way down the steps. He was unshaven, shiny faced, radiating fermented body odor. I got two beers from the fridge, and when I handed one to him, he stared at me, pinched disbelief in his eyes. "I thought you were going to decorate this place," he said.

Boxes were stacked in the corners, and the walls were bare. I could live that way for years, getting things out as I needed them.

"I'm not much of a housekeeper, I guess," I said.

He shook his head in disgust and stared over my shoulder. "You said you would," he said, under his breath.

Had I? I barely even listened to my promises anymore. I said, "Well."

"This place is a *shithole*," he whispered.

He handed me back the beer, and clomped up the steps.

When my father died, he left no will. Three mortgages on the house. No life insurance. Four hundred and twenty-one dollars in the savings account that Mom thought was a thousand times that. Five credit cards, maxed out. Mom couldn't make even the first mortgage payment after he was gone.

Soon, we had moved from Lake Forest to Libertyville, to a two-bedroom rental where we had to share a bathroom. Mom did a lot of weeping over money then, and for a while it pissed me off that Dad had been reduced to this — to his financial profile. Our grief was all about money — all about the cable we couldn't afford, the summer job I needed to get, the bus pass we shared, the skeezy people on the bus who scared Mom. What about Dad? I wanted to shout. But that didn't last long. Because what about him? There was the old Dad — sometimes a good guy, sometimes a mean one, usually half-drunk, but always, always a man with a dollar in his pocket, a picker-upper of checks, someone who paid top dollar for the best things and then told you about it — and then there was the deadbeat we never knew.

I hated being poor, almost as much as Mom did. That hatred has lasted longer than anything else, longer than any feeling for Dad, any feeling for Mom, any feeling for good old Chicago, city of the big whatever — it lasted all the way til now. Where's my inheritance, is what I'd like to know. I can hardly bear to pay a bill. I cash those sad little paychecks, and I want to keep every penny.

In this, I'm like the landlord. I want my money, too.

I started to feel him watching. Curtains inched apart in his windows when I left or returned. He'd stand in the weedy backyard, smoking and staring at the building. Once I heard him yelling at the women across the street, ranting about witchcraft.

I started to feel that we were all alone out here on the edge of town. Me and the landlord and those silent other homes on the cul-de-sac. And the empty lots, the places where homes were supposed to go before it became apparent that there just wasn't much desire to be here.

I left my job as a till monkey at 7-Eleven after the manager developed an attitude about my punctuality.

"I think we're going to need to make this formal," he said after a rambling discourse on the need for on-time performance. "I think we're going to need to write this up."

"Why don't you write this up?" I suggested, and I lifted one hind cheek off the cheap plastic seat. But I could summon no percussion. Story of my etc. It's disappointing to come so near a high point and miss it — the kind of moment they write country songs about, or epic poems. *And then he made a trumpet of his ass.* I leveled my trumpet back into the seat and said, "I quit."

He couldn't have been happier.

I drove home and sat on the hood of the Fiesta in the driveway. I was almost three months behind on the rent, and this new development seemed to suggest a change. Maybe I could head to Seattle and try panhandling. Or hire myself out on a ship. With my absence of seafaring skills, I could accept a competitive wage. The vistas were wide, wide open, like the view from the middle of the ocean.

I wondered if the landlord was in my apartment at that very moment. If he was, then OK. I'd give him time to get out. That was not my place. It was just somewhere I would leave in the middle of the night. It was midafternoon, a June day drying out the rain. Earthworms, bloated and pink, were dying on the road.

"Hey!"

I jumped so hard I slid from the hood of the Fiesta. The landlord had shuffled up behind me.

"When am I gonna get my money?"

I hadn't seen him in days. His hair had seemingly become whiter and his face redder. His breath was ragged and furious. This is it, I thought. Here comes the heave-ho.

"Jesus, you scared me," I said.

"I want my fucking money," he said, his voice a low tremor. His mouth seemed full of pebbles, and his eyes raced in tiny circles in the air behind me. He said, "Sweet Lord," and stiffened. His eyes widened, and he said it again, "Sweet Lord," but his throat closed on the words like a fist, and the burgundy in his face deepened. His body, his huge carcass, clenched and fell. He landed on his side, grunting quietly, and his left foot moved as though he were trying to spin himself on the concrete.

I'm no doctor, but it seemed bad. It seemed like a heart attack, a big one, not one of those shortness-of-breath, pain-in-the-arm things. I was disgusted — this belonged out of sight, where the rest of us didn't have to see it. My dead father crowded into the moment, forever fifty-one, forever a man who'd failed to keep a will and made less money than he let on.

I ran to the duplex at the end of the cul-de-sac, and felt my rickety knees and the slide of my belly, and tried to remember when I had last run. I was already exhausted after climbing the steps to the top unit. No one answered there so I tried downstairs, and no one answered there, either. I was coated in slick perspiration, sweat tingling on my scalp, snaking down behind my ears and collecting along the waistband of my jeans. I ran to the house across

the street, the one with the surveilling witches, and before I got to the door, I shifted down to a fast walk, gasp-
ing, and no one answered there, either. I walked an ordinary
walk back across the street to the driveway where the landlord lay on his side, motionless now. I saw that his cheek
rested on a few pebbles and no breath rose from his slack
mouth.

I could have driven for help. I could have done that.

I spun around slowly, looking carefully in every direction,
and then walked into my apartment. I left off all the lights. I
didn't open a shade. I grabbed my headlamp and some magazines and my copy of *Notes from Underground,* and I went
into the closet and pulled the doors closed behind me. I sat
on the floor. I was there for hours before I heard some com-
motion outside, and in those hours I ached with the wish
that I would never see another human being, that my life
from then on would be silent and rich with darkness, and
then slowly, once again, I stopped wishing it.

When I went out, it was about eight, heading into the final hour of daylight, and the ambulance was parked at the
end of the driveway. Medics were hauling the landlord onto
a stretcher, and three young women stood a few yards away,
watching and talking behind their hands. I walked over. One
of them wore running shorts and a tight top. The other two
were in sweatpants and T-shirts.

The runner, the blondest of them, asked me if I lived in
the duplex, and I said I did. I told them I'd had no idea what
happened until I heard the ambulance.

"I saw him there when I came out for my run," she said. "It was awful. He must have been there for hours."

I said, "I was inside the whole time."

The other girl said, "Wild."

Two young guys in white shirts and ties, all bright faced and clean, rode up on bicycles and asked if there was anything they could do to help. One of the women rolled her eyes at them, and they rode off. The women said they'd never spoken to the landlord. They said it was tragic to live so close to your neighbors without even knowing each other.

"Or maybe it's not so tragic," I said.

"What's that supposed to mean?" the runner asked.

I thought about shrugging, then didn't. After a pause, they shook their heads and turned to go.

It was about dark. The single streetlight at the end of the cul-de-sac came on, a sickly yellow. I walked toward my apartment, but instead of going down the stairs, I went up, to the landlord's door. I put my hand on his doorknob and with a half turn could feel it was unlocked. I let go, and for the second time that day I did a guilty scan of the neighborhood.

Nobody was watching.

I opened the door and went in. The air had a trapped smell, like unfamiliar food burned long ago. As my eyes adjusted, gray shapes came into view: his couch, the television reflecting the room, a lamp, an empty vase. I pulled open his refrigerator, and an obscene light spread into the room. On the wire shelves sat cans of food — chili, corned beef hash — with pieces of aluminum foil molded over the tops. A lonely box of baking soda. Leaving the fridge door open for light, I looked around. A sleek telephone, forest green, hung from the wall, its twisted cord dangling like a tail. I picked up the phone and dialed Mom's number in Illinois.

The answering machine. My voice on the message, three years old: "Hi. Sorry. Leave a number."

I felt a flare of hatred for that earlier me, the one trapped in time and about to be forgotten by his mother. I didn't leave a message, and she didn't answer, but sometimes it took her a while to get to the phone, so I hung up and dialed again, and the machine picked up a second time.

I listened to several seconds of silence after the beep.

I shouted, "I'm in Idaho!"

I hung up. I looked at the books on the landlord's shelves. Louis L'Amour. Ayn Rand. Other stuff I hated. I sat on the couch. Then I lay down, adjusting a pillow under my head. Sleep came like a drug and I drank it, held it to my chest and sank with it, until I was gone.

Winter Elders

THEY MATERIALIZED WITH the first snow. That was how Bradshaw would always remember it. He was standing at the living-room window, listening to Cheryl shush the baby, when he saw specks fluttering like ash against a smoky sky, then caught sight of someone on his front step, though he hadn't noticed anyone coming up the walk. He could see about an inch of a man's left side at the window's border — an arm in a dark suit and a boyish hand holding a book bound in black leather. He knew instantly that there was another suit and another leather-bound volume out there, a companion to complete the pair: missionaries.

Bradshaw opened the door and blocked the frame. Body language was everything. Announce it — *you're not coming in.* On the step were two kids in suits, short hair, name tags. One was tall — taller than Bradshaw, maybe six foot four — and the baby fat on his face had begun to jowlify. The shorter one was younger, with avid eyes and scraped cheeks.

"Brother Bradshaw?" the tall one asked as he looked into the house. "Hi, we're here from the Church."

"I can see that."

"We're just wanting to check in, see if there's anything we can do for you."

"You could clean out my gutters," Bradshaw said. "Or rake the yard."

The little one chuckled, but the tall one looked up at the gutters, spilling over with leaves and twigs. The falling snow had thickened.

"Don't think we won't," he said.

His name tag read *Elder Pope*. He would not drop his smile or avert his eyes. There was something stubborn in him and, deeper, the sense that he was proud of his stubbornness. Bradshaw was impressed, a little.

"After you're done you could change the oil in my car," Bradshaw said. "So long as you're just wanting to help."

Elder Pope nodded softly, and pointed with his chin toward the inside of the house.

"Maybe we could come in and discuss your list of chores," he said.

"Right," Bradshaw said.

The littler missionary — his name tag read *Elder Warren* — said, "Could we just talk to you for a few minutes about Jesus Christ?"

"You could not just talk to me for a few minutes about Jesus Christ," Bradshaw said, pushing the door closed slowly against Pope's cheer. "I'd like it if you stopped coming here. Make a note back at the coven."

Through the window in the door, Bradshaw saw Warren turn to go, but Pope stayed, staring for a few seconds.

Bradshaw was twelve years out of the church and not going back. For a long time, a new set of missionaries had appeared every few months, cloaked in fresh optimism. Each time, Bradshaw's hunger to disappoint them had deepened, until he finally asked them to remove him from the Church rolls for good. To kick him out. It had taken months, but they finally sent him a letter of excommunication, revoking his baptismal blessings and eternal privileges as a member of the Church of Jesus Christ of Latter-day Saints. The letter read like a credit-card cancellation, and he and Cheryl had made much fun of it. "You're out!" she would say and wrap her arms around his neck, and though he was glad to be out, too, her reaction made him defensive, and he would feel a germ of insult stick and grow. Now, staring at the place in the storm where the missionaries had vanished, he wished he'd asked what brought them back this time.

He heard the baby crying and went to check on him. He found Cheryl bouncing the boy gently, whispering, "And then the pig decided to become a happy pig and spread happiness into the world . . ."

"Who was it?" she whispered.

"Missionaries."

"You've got to be kidding," she said, bugging her eyes while she swayed and rubbed the baby's back.

"I'm not kidding."

Bradshaw leaned toward the boy and whispered, "Hello, Riley. Hello, Brother Bradshaw."

Cheryl pulled the boy away.

"Don't," she said. "That's not funny."

She was always serious now. Ever since the baby. *Earnest*. Riley was nine months old, and Bradshaw wondered what had happened to his partner in cynicism. They used to be in complete agreement about this if nothing else: Everything was such bullshit. Everything was so ridiculous. They had been bloodhounds for any trace of sentiment, any note of sincerity, upon which to pounce mockingly; after parties, they competed to do the best eviscerating impressions, and new parents, all wide-eyed and self-absorbed, had been a specialty of Cheryl's. Such bullshit, people and their human mess. Now Bradshaw felt abandoned, adrift in his own head and swamped with hot-eyed exhaustion. The boy had started sleeping most of the night, usually waking just once, fussing and whimpering until Cheryl nursed him back to sleep. Bradshaw knew he had it easy by comparison, but still he felt flocked by trouble. Besieged. Once awakened, he would lie there for an hour or more, mind fixed on his current aggravation — an argument at work, something Cheryl had said, some spot of tension with the world. He would dream his constant dream of putting people in their place. Sometimes he lay on his side and watched the boy's head bob as he nursed, and Bradshaw would feel once more the pressure that had arrived with the child — a relentless sense that he was not up to this. That he was not made to be a father.

Coming home from work four days later, Bradshaw swung his car into the driveway, and the headlights washed over two spectral shapes in the grainy dusk. The missionaries. Pope had his hand wrapped around a rake shaft, talking to Warren, who was looking up and nodding. The snow had melted, and gluey brown leaves had been raked into a pile.

The open garage door spread a fan of warm light, but the house was dark. Cheryl and Riley were at her sister's. Bradshaw slammed his car door and only then did Pope look up, lifting his arm in an exaggerated wave, as though he were on a dock greeting a steamer.

"Brother Bradshaw!" he said. "Good evening."

Warren raised a hand briefly. He wore his embarrassment like a shawl.

Bradshaw stepped off the driveway onto the wet lawn, cold air like metal in his sinuses. The rake had been in the garage. They had gone into the garage.

"I bet you never thought we'd take you up on it," Pope said, smiling even as Bradshaw grabbed the rake handle and jerked. Pope held firm for a second, smile widening — in surprise or malevolence, Bradshaw couldn't tell — then let go, sending Bradshaw backward one step. Pope shrugged sheepishly.

"Sorry," he said.

Warren laughed, snuffling behind his hand. Did he say something? Something to Pope? Bradshaw stared, seething. Breath crowded his lungs, and his vision tightened and blurred. Pope smiled patiently at Bradshaw, lips pressed hammily together. It was the smile of every man he had met in church, the bishops and first counselors and stake presidents, the benevolent mask, the put-on solemnity, the utter falseness. It was the smile of the men who brought boxes of food when Bradshaw was a teenager and his father wasn't working, the canned meat and bricks of cheese. The men who prayed for his family. Bradshaw's father would disappear, leaving him and his mother to kneel with the men.

Setting the rake against his shoulder, Bradshaw ground the heels of his hands into his eyes. When he opened them, red spots expanded and danced across his vision. The missionaries faded, then clarified.

"Brother Bradshaw?" Pope said.

Bradshaw wanted to swing the rake at Pope's head. To watch his smug eyes pop as the tines sunk in. Why could he not just do it? He never could. Finally, he simply pointed toward the road, eyes averted, finger trembling. As they left, Pope said without looking back, "We'll be praying for you, Brother Bradshaw."

Bradshaw threw down the rake.

"Don't pray for me!" he shouted. "Don't you *dare* pray for me!"

He stopped when he saw his neighbor, Bud Swenson, standing at his mailbox, a handful of envelopes.

Later, after Cheryl returned, he sat on the floor with Riley, trying to get him interested in stacking wooden blocks. It was Tuesday of Thanksgiving week, and Cheryl was making pie crusts. She came in and watched them a moment, and when Bradshaw looked up, wooden block in hand, he was startled to find her on the verge of happy tears. It reminded him of the way his mother would get in church, swept up in the spirit.

"I still can't believe you want to do the whole Thanksgiving thing," Bradshaw said. "With a baby."

"I know," she said. "But I want to. I feel like we're finally a family."

"We are finally a family," he said. "But so what?"

When the boy was born, Bradshaw kept waiting for it to happen. The flash of light. The surge of joy. Some brightness shining through the visible world. He had been so sure this would be it — the moment that he felt what everyone else seemed to feel, what his mother felt, what all the other Mormons felt, what people in other churches felt, what even people like Cheryl felt, people who were hostile to the very idea of religion: some spirit in the material. The thing behind the thing. Cheryl called it "an animating force."

"There has to be something, doesn't there?" she said. "When you really think about it? Something larger than us?"

Sometimes he thought she was right, and sometimes he thought she was wrong, and the fact that he could not decide had given him a sense that he was failing a fundamental duty to believe. In something or nothing. He had always been that way — back as far as he could remember, his mind fixed on the yes or no of it, and always shifting. He recalled wondering, when he was baptized at age eight, why all these spiritual people needed a mime show like baptism. Instead of anything transcendent, he had felt awakened to the concrete moment — the water in the font, the thick wet of the baptismal garment.

As a teenager, at church camp, he had watched as the boys and girls stood up at testimony meeting and swore they had faith in the Lord, that they had a testimony this was the true church. They wept and trembled, one after another, and soon he stood too and choked on his tears, swore he had been given a testimony. It was as though a bright beam of joy was pulsing from the heavens into the core of the earth, threaded directly through him. But by that night, he felt it fading, and within days it was gone. He told himself that what had happened was not genuine, that he had simply been weak, swept up.

When Riley was born, the moment assaulted him in its earthbound reality — the blood and mucus under the bright lights of the delivery room, the boy's pinched eyes, magenta skin, clammy hair, and that cord, that bunched gray-

red tube of matter and fluid. It arrived like a undeniable announcement — this moment is the one thing. His son struck
him not as an angel or a spirit, but as an animal, a creature
who would die without his care, a creature who would die,
a creature bound to other creatures. Bradshaw pressed the
scissors and the blades separated the boy from his mother.

Later, Cheryl told him she'd been overwhelmed by something she could not define. "Just some kind of . . . whatever," she said, and laughed. In the first days of it, when they
would find themselves up at three a.m., waiting for Riley to
stop gurgling in the bassinette, she would talk about it.

"Isn't it crazy?" she said, in a whisper of wonder. "It really
is a miracle. It really is what people say."

She waited for him to answer. A pale parallelogram of
summer moonlight lay over the closet door; he could smell
cut grass outside, the cool of a sprinkler. What could he
tell her? That he felt like he was being filled with life and
drained of life all at once? That he had not imagined the con-
suming force of it? That he ached for the way he used to be
filled with himself, only himself, all Bradshaw?

"A miracle," he said. "It really is."

The day after Thanksgiving, it snowed almost a foot. Everything rounded, muffled. Snow balanced in strips along fence
tops and tree limbs; footsteps left deep wells across lawns.
It snowed another five inches overnight, and the next day
dawned bright and icy. That afternoon, Bradshaw shov-
eled the walk for the third time in two days. His neighbor

Bud Swenson's German shepherd, Jake, a genial but blood-thirsty-looking dog, came over to be petted. He and Bud shouted pleasantries and shared weather statistics. Bradshaw heard footsteps squeaking and scrunching around the corner. Later he would think he had sensed the missionaries' appearance before they appeared, trudging down his street since half the sidewalks were unshoveled.

Bradshaw took Jake by the collar, bent down and whispered in his ear, "Go get 'em, boy. Sic 'em, Jakie," and the dog braced. Bud called, "You're not telling him any of my secrets are ya?" and laughed, and Bradshaw ignored him and watched the missionaries approach. They did not angle toward his walkway, but kept to the road, and as they drew closer Pope raised a hand and shouted, "Hello, Brother Bradshaw," and Bradshaw said, "Sic 'em, boy!" Jake shot off, barking ferociously, while Bud shouted at him to stop.

Pope scrambled back, slipping, but Warren stood in place. He held out one hand, palm down, and said, "Hey there. Good boy. Good boy. That's a good boy," in a soothing voice. The dog stopped a few feet from Warren and kept barking.

"Hey, there, you're a good boy," Warren said.

He brought his other hand from his coat pocket and presented it, palm up. The dog stopped barking. His tail began to wag. He stepped toward the missionary and started to eat from his hand. Bradshaw stared. His stomach splashed like a boisterous sea. Warren patted the dog on the head, and the dog looked back at Bradshaw, tongue out, tail whipping the frigid air.

Bud called, "Come here, dammit," and glared at Bradshaw. The dog obeyed. Pope and Warren stood looking back and forth between Bradshaw and Bud, and when Bud shook his head and went toward his house, the missionaries turned and approached Bradshaw. He thought what he was feeling then — ribs like hot, heavy irons in his chest — was despair, true despair in the face of the grinding, unbeatable world.

"Missionaries always carry dog treats," Pope said, smiling once again.

Bradshaw said, "Look," and Pope stepped to him, face bright with cold.

"May I ask you a favor, Brother Bradshaw? I know this sounds crazy, given everything, but could we possibly come into your home for a moment and warm up? That's all — just warm up? We're awfully cold right now, and my companion here is in worse shape than me."

Warren shivered, and his bright nose dripped. Bradshaw felt weakened by the demand. What kind of person was he, that he wanted so badly to say no?

"OK," he said, turning and heading up the walk. Inside, they stood on the entry rug, in coats and hats, ringed by a dusting of snow.

"I'll be right back," Bradshaw said, and went to the baby's room. Cheryl was sitting by the rocker, reading a magazine while Riley napped. When Bradshaw told her what he'd done, she rolled her eyes and said, "It's your mess." He returned to the living room and saw the missionaries standing there, still bundled up. They seemed small. Young.

"Why don't you sit down for a second?" Bradshaw asked.

Warren dragged a glove across his nose. Pope unzipped his coat and pulled off his hat. They unsheathed and sat down on his couch, and Bradshaw sat in a chair.

"Don't get any ideas," he said.

"Well," Pope said. "I wonder if I might ask you just one question."

Unbelievable. "You might," he said.

Cheryl had moved to the dining room. He could hear her clicking on a calculator, tearing off checks.

"I just wonder if you've ever read the Book of Mormon all the way through and prayed about it?" Pope said. "Just gave it one real chance."

The question shocked Bradshaw. He'd come to feel that it wasn't what Pope was up to, after all. That he was here for something else.

"I don't . . ." He couldn't figure out how to begin. "No, I haven't. I mean — you know what I think about when I think about the Church? The stupid seagulls." Bradshaw hadn't really thought about the seagulls in years. "How those bugs were eating all the pioneers' crops and great clouds of seagulls came and ate them up. Right? In Salt Lake? Saved everybody from starving? Divine intervention?"

"What do you think about it?" Pope asked.

"What a bunch of bullshit it is. I mean, birds eat bugs."

"I had some relatives there for that," Warren said. "Ancestors."

"Yeah? OK. Whatever. Let's just say it's a nice story. A nice little *tale*."

Pope seemed confused. "Just keep an open mind, is all I'm saying."

"That'd be a bit too open for me," Bradshaw said, and now he was feeling better, kind of energized. "I mean, actually, that'd be way, way too open."

The gears in Pope's smile slipped. Bradshaw continued, "Really, guys, that book is no more an ancient record than I am the Duke of Scotland," and the air in his lungs felt good again, "Maybe *you'd* like to keep an open mind to a few things. The historical record, for instance . . ."

A gate unlocked inside him. The beasts trampled out.

"I mean, right there on the first page or two, you've got a guy named Sam. Sam!" he said. His voice felt harsh and spiny in his throat. He was thinking that he'd really start — really blast every story about Joseph Smith, about the "translation" of the Book of Mormon, about everything. Make the stupid fuckers see.

"Sam! Sam! Just some Central American dude, 2,000 years ago, named Sam! Not Quetzalcoatl or some shit. Sam!" He couldn't stop saying it. Fury tightened his scalp, the sockets of his eyes.

A long wail came from the back bedroom. Bradshaw stopped and realized how loud he'd been. He looked at Warren, gazing forlornly at his hands. Pope kept his eyes on Bradshaw, looking resigned and sad. Bradshaw heard

Cheryl stand and walk to the nursery. Hard, angry steps. He sat hot faced and trembly, embarrassment seeping in. The baby stopped crying, and still no one spoke.

Cheryl walked into the room, gently rocking the boy.

"I don't want you people in my house," she said, in her quiet-baby hush. "My husband can't seem to tell you that, but I'm telling you now. If you come back again, I'm going to call the police. I'll get a restraining order."

Warren said, "Yes, ma'am," and Pope's eyes bored into the floor. They rose and shuffled toward the door. Drew on their coats and hats. Warren stepped out, but Pope stopped and looked at Bradshaw.

"I just want to say, before I leave you alone," he whispered, "that I know the gospel is true. I know it. I know that it is true because God has told me it is true, and not because I'm special, or different than anyone else on this earth, but because He loves us all, all of us, all His children, and He will give us this knowledge if we ask Him for it. I promise you that, Brother Bradshaw. I swear it."

Pope, flushed and wet eyed, ducked his head and left. Bradshaw felt an emotional swell that recalled that day when he had stood before the others at church camp and wept. It was not that Pope was right and he was wrong, and not that Pope was wrong and he was right. It was that Pope had something he could not have, and he would spend his life not having it.

• • •

The snow refused to stop. Berms piled head high. Enormous icicles grew down from gutters to the ground. Bradshaw was shoveling the walk one night when he heard someone shout, "Hello!" He looked up and saw two shapes across the street, passing out of the streetlight and into the gray mist. One tall, one short. Both turned their shadowed faces to him as they passed.

The next night, dropping cans and newspaper into the re-cycling bin, he thought he saw a figure move behind a tree in his side yard. He walked toward it, stepping into calf-deep snow in his slippers. He thought he heard the soft crunch of a footstep.

"Pope!" he whispered harshly. "You better not let me find you out here."

Bradshaw's words billowed before him.

"I will make you wish you'd never been born."

Silence, but for the radical drumming of his heart.

"You're going to be in a world of hurt."

These were things Bradshaw's father used to say when he was angry, and they were things that Bradshaw had fanta-sized about saying to others, as his stronger self. His fantasy self.

"I swear to God I'll stomp a mudhole in your ass."

Bradshaw's father had only mentioned God when he was issuing a threat. His mom had dragged them all to church on Sundays, to the tan brick ward house on Main Street. Everyone could tell his dad wasn't a part of it, just by the way he stared out windows or into walls. After his mom died and he lived with his father in a downtown apartment, they stopped going to church altogether. When the men from the ward came on Sundays to visit, his father wouldn't answer the door. They would sit inside, hold their breath, and wait for the footsteps to disappear down the hall.

"Pope," Bradshaw whispered, shivering, feet and legs soaked. "Pope."

Snowflakes began to fall. Bradshaw looked up into the purple sky, the glowing winter night. Snow plunged and swerved downward, and he felt drawn upward into a dark heaven. He was weightless. He would never stomp a mudhole in anyone's ass.

The next morning, before work, Bradshaw walked to the pine trees in the side yard — the huge, sixty-year-old tree and the littler pine tucked against it. The snow was sunken with footprints, drifted over by snow, crisscrossing, back and forth. He could not tell where they came from or where they were going.

Riley woke the next day with a fever, cranky and wailing. Bradshaw tried to take his temperature under his arm, but he wouldn't stay still.

"Maybe we ought to try the rectal thermometer," Cheryl said.

"Maybe you ought to try the rectal thermometer," Bradshaw said. He put his hand on the baby's forehead. "He doesn't feel *that* hot."

By the time Bradshaw returned from work, the boy was blazing: 101, 102. He wouldn't take breast or bottle. His diaper had been dry for hours. He was radiant in Bradshaw's arms. Cheryl looked as if she hadn't left his room all day — still in her sweatpants and T-shirt, fretful and pale.

"This is getting worse, right?" Bradshaw said.

"I think so. I'm not sure."

Bradshaw cupped the boy's head in his palm. It felt like a stone on a riverbank, some noon in July. Riley wouldn't stop whimpering and fidgeting, rubbing his soft fingers around his face. Cheryl tried to give him a dropper full of pink Tylenol, but he spat it out.

"What did the doctor say?" Bradshaw asked.

"Come in if it gets worse."

"This is worse. I think it's worse."

"We should go. Shouldn't we go?"

Bradshaw drove slowly on the snow-packed roads, leaning forward with both hands on the wheel. About halfway there, three large snowflakes landed on the windshield and melted.

"It can't snow anymore," Cheryl said. "It can't."

At the hospital, the ER nurse said, "Oh dear, this little guy's dehydrated," and they hooked him up to an IV. The sight of the needle invading his son's arm, of the dry skin cracking his lower lip, made Bradshaw feel helpless — proof that he was being tasked beyond his capabilities. Cheryl hustled around the room, checking the diaper bag for wipes, watching Riley's skin color, rushing out to the nurses with questions. Bradshaw sat beside the boy, sliding crushed ice into his mouth. Soon, Riley was cooler and calmer, but the doctor wanted to keep him overnight, so Bradshaw left to get toothbrushes and underwear.

Outside, new snow was piling onto old. Cars stuck at stoplights, spinning as the lights went green. Bradshaw drove slowly along the busy arterial. When he got to his neighborhood, he built up as much speed as he could before turning onto the unplowed street, but he immediately bogged down. Halfway up the block, he spun to a stop and sat there, breathing loudly, mind hurtling — the boy would be OK, no thanks to him. But Riley's illness, his frailty and animal need, had sent an exact message: If the boy died — not now, he was not dying now, Bradshaw knew — Bradshaw would die, as well. Not that he would kill himself, though he thought he would, but that he had become something else entirely, a new being who would only exist so long as his son existed. If the boy died, Bradshaw would become a ghost. He sat in his car as his breath fogged the windshield. He would never be free. He tried to slow his breathing and could not.

He climbed out, locked the car, and started walking the five blocks home. The storm blew sideways. Flakes clung to his eyelashes and nostrils. Trudging clumsily in his snow boots, he was exhausted by the time he reached his house, dark and unlit. He started up the sidewalk, and a voice came from the darkness. "Hey there, Brother Bradshaw."

Bradshaw stopped. He looked at his house and couldn't see Pope anywhere.

"Sorry to surprise you like this," the voice said.

It was coming from the edge of the front patio, from the two metal chairs they never used. Bradshaw stared, narrowed his eyes. He thought he saw a shape in one of the chairs. He took several slow steps toward it.

"Pope?"

"Who else?"

Now the shape seemed to be standing. He could hear Pope smiling. Bradshaw was glad he had returned. Furiously thrilled. He took another step, and noticed that someone had cleared the snow from the fake rock where they hid the spare key. The fake rock lay overturned, a bowl filling with snow.

"I need to come in, Brother Bradshaw."

"You're not coming in."

"I need to come in."

The shape and the voice seemed to separate.

"Where's your partner?"

"He's home. Sick," Pope scoffed.

"What are you doing out?"

"Knocking on doors." The shape hung before him, straight ahead on the walk, grainy, slowly growing into Pope in the weak light. "Doing the Lord's work. But I'm awfully cold now, Brother Bradshaw. I need to come in."

"You're not coming in."

Pope held up the spare key between the fingers of his glove.

"I'm coming in. You know it. You do. It's just another

thing you're not letting yourself believe right now. But you know it. In your heart."

"Nobody knows shit with their heart, Pope. That's not what the heart does."

Pope sighed, a long weary breath that turned smoky in the air.

"People are always telling me no, Brother Bradshaw. All day long. Do you have any idea how discouraging that is?"

He turned toward the door, and Bradshaw lunged, wrapping his arms around Pope's torso. It didn't feel like something he'd actually done — it didn't feel like anything he would ever do. He scrabbled for the key, but Pope twisted and fought. Hanging on from behind, Bradshaw drove him onto the snowy sidewalk, feeling his rib cage expand with every breath. Pope fought to his knees, and they lumbered and lurched, and Bradshaw found his right hand suddenly, accidentally, clamped over Pope's mouth, bony chin snug in his grip.

"OK," Pope said, relaxing. "All right."

Bradshaw's body wanted to do it. That was how he would always remember it — his body did it without him. His muscles twitched and fluttered with desire. His bones gathered and heaved backward. The sound was horrendous — a crack like a tree limb splitting — and Bradshaw felt it in his muscles and bones, in his own neck.

He sat back as Pope slumped onto his face, rear in the air like a sleeping toddler. Bradshaw breathed and breathed, watching each white cloud rise. Pope didn't move. Snow soaked through Bradshaw's pants. He stood. He noticed he didn't feel surprised. He hadn't expected this, but now that he was in the middle of it, it didn't feel unexpected.

"You're not coming in," Bradshaw whispered.

He leaned over and removed the key from Pope's glove, and used it to open the front door. He went in, took off his boots and coat, and began turning on lights. He walked the house, flipping every switch, every lamp, the bathroom lights, garage light, pouring on light. He stood in the blazing yellow of his front-room window and gazed at the dark shape in the snow. He raised a force field around his mind and kept everything outside of it — wife and child, mother and father, the idea that the sun would rise on him ever again. He thought: I could eat a whole chicken. Or a pizza. The snow fell and fell on Pope, and Bradshaw watched it and thought: I'm either damned or I'm not, but I am *starving*.

He went to the kitchen. He found ham and turkey and Irish farmhouse cheese in the fridge, and made a thick, chewy sandwich. Lots of mayonnaise. No vegetables. His mouth was dry, and he had a hard time choking down the first bite.

"Not coming in!" he said, spraying crumbs and bits of half-chewed meat.

It was a delicious sandwich. He took another bite, but it turned impossible in his parched mouth, and he spat it onto the counter, a fleshy lump. He'd have to clean this up before he called the police. "A *hell* of a sandwich!" he said. He was holding it in both hands, staring at the empty places he had bitten away. He walked toward the front of the house. He had a vision of himself welcoming the officers. His demeanor would be pitched perfectly. Just the way Pope would do it. It would be no time for smiling. Whatever he said would be believable.

Opposition in All Things

I

THEN I AWOKE. Sea the color of stone curled away in every direction, tucking itself beneath a bright mist that blotted out the sky. A tinge of lilac bleeding into the frosty air. A rocking, a lulling. Was this the celestial kingdom? I had believed I was dying into God's glory. Now I was seeing through someone else's eyes, and could but hope this was a passage, a way there. The ashen sea rocked on. I stared into the haze, longing to see it open upon a wide shore, a sacred light, the heavenly host.

But the mist did not part and no shore appeared and I remained behind the eyes of a stranger, a sailor on an armored warship, standing ready beside a big gun on the foredeck, a bigger gun than I had ever seen. I watched with him from the deck, and from his seat at the mess, and as he read his letters in his cramped bunk, sour water swishing on the floor below. It was no heaven and no hell, and soon I realized, from the letters, that he was no stranger. He was Rulon Warren, the son of a niece whom I had only known as a girl. And what was I? Angel or spirit? And what was my purpose?

When we returned from the war in Europe and all we had seen there, Rulon Warren wanted nothing but the silence no one would allow. He was assaulted by talk. Everyone called for an accounting. I wanted so much to help him then, to ease his way or strike down his enemies, but I held no such earthly powers.

His parents wanted to speak to him at all hours — his mother, my niece, about church services and socials, young women in town, his plans for the future; his father about the barley, canal weeds, young women in town. His mother could talk for hours, it seemed, while his father spoke only three and four words at a time, but they both wanted the same from him, a future parceled out in syllables.

At church on Sundays, the older men came up one by one, shy, like courters at a dance. *Didn't it make you seasick, all that time on the boat? How many of those Huns did you send into outer darkness?* Rulon sometimes could not think of a single word. He would blush and shrug and look at the ward-house floor, and the men would do something similar, rebuked. They'd pat him on the shoulder and retreat. Other times the answers came as if from another place. He was never once seasick. "Best sea legs on the ship came from right here in Idaho," he'd brag. And in his job on the ship, navigating the fixed gun on the foredeck, he'd probably helped kill thirty-five or forty of the kaiser's boys. "My share," he would say, and try to smile. "Maybe a few more."

I could feel his temptation to tell them, the men with their fingernails cleaned and hair slick for Sunday, that he'd stood next to a gunner whose head had vanished in a pink mist, and that hours later, belowdecks and pulsing with adrenaline, he had found bits of skull clinging to the shoulder of his uniform. Or that he had watched as his fellow sailors fired on the survivors of the *Gotthilf*, the destroyer they'd sunk in the metal-gray North Sea, the Germans bobbing in the water, waving their arms in surrender, and then jerking and sliding below the churning water while the sailors laughed. I could feel Rulon's desire to unsettle the brethren, to terrify them — it was the selfsame desire I had brought to church during my own life, Sunday after Sunday, and in those early days of our coexistence it made me feel we were aligned.

And yet we were not. Rulon's guilt boiled at him. He pitied those Huns, which had struck me as weak when he'd first felt it, out on the ship. Like the response of a child. I had only recently joined him then and was lost inside my new existence. I had died, bleeding onto the earth in the Tetons, killed by a posse, and then thirty-two years passed in a black instant and I awoke inside Rulon's vision. We were sailing into a sea that spread in every direction into a cloak of fog. The bliss of death was already fading, and the first sensations of my new life were the salt air, the roll of the horizon, the anxiety burning within Rulon, and the fear that I had awakened to something never-ending.

Weeks later, after I had discovered, from his letters, the passage of time since my death, Rulon couldn't let the deaths of those Huns go. He would pray at night for forgiveness, and he dwelled upon the souls of the Germans, pondering how their eternities would be affected by their foreshortened lives. What if they had died before they'd had the chance to achieve their full righteousness? He worried about his own sin as well, and I was there with him in all of it. I saw what he saw, and I sensed his thoughts and shared in the images that spun relentlessly through his mind. He thought back to the time, before he had shipped, when he'd asked the bishop whether it was a sin to kill an enemy in warfare. Bishop Lawton, a short, thin man who curved forward at the shoulders, had seemed surprised.

"You're serving your country, son," he said. "That's no sin."

Then the bishop cited the warfare in the Bible, the battles in the Book of Mormon between Nephites and Lamanites. The sixth commandment was a prohibition on murder, he said, not war. As Rulon brooded, I thought of my own life — my desire to be exalted for slaying the Lord's enemies and my fear that I would be damned instead. I now doubted that either was true. Was this damnation? Exaltation? I could see no punishment in it, nor any reward. When Rulon prayed in his bunk at night, doubt hounded my thoughts. What was this life? Where was God's hand?

When I had been alive, I prayed daily, over meals and with my parents and sister, and by myself before bed. I prayed before every decision. I prayed before asking Sally Bartram to marry, and then we prayed together once she said yes. I prayed before I bought my own cattle — the fifteen head my father told me I was a fool to purchase. The cattle sold at a profit, and I knew that I would discard the wisdom of my elders and listen only for the answers to my prayers. I prayed when I left the church and my parents and faithless Sally Bartram, and I received an answer, the knowledge that I was walking in the Lord's light. I'd known it then the way I knew how to strike with a maul or knot a length of rope, but I did not know it any longer. Every new day showed me that I must have been wrong. Rulon would get no help from beyond but for me, and I pitied us both.

In his bunk on the ship, Rulon had often wondered why no one else was concerned about the killing. The whole town of Franklin, it seemed, had come to wish him farewell when he left for the navy. They had all appeared happy he was going, so proud. He fretted over these memories, unable to overcome his fear that everyone — the ward, the town, the whole country — was wrong about this: *Thou shalt not kill,* he thought. They had papered over sin with happy lies.

Now that he was back, the bishop was after him to give a talk to the ward. Rulon could share how the Lord had helped him through his times at sea. "Maybe not yet," Rulon said, but what he did not say was that he had experienced no help from the Lord at sea. He had ridden on that ship beyond the sight of land and beyond the hand of the Lord, which he had not thought possible.

He returned certain he was fallen.

All that talk. How I wished to draw a curtain of silence around him. To describe for him the eternity of silence awaiting him, how comforting it might be before it turned to torment. To say: *Peace be with you.* To say: *May peace cast its shadow on your heart.* But my words weighed nothing, and even then — when I still wanted him to live — I had no honest desire for peace.

Rulon had been honorably discharged in May 1918 and had spent a week in San Francisco with some of the other men from the USS *Gooding.* At night he had stayed in his hotel room, paid for by the navy, and had tried to adjust to the idea that he was back in this world. San Francisco was as foreign as the sea. Sailors roamed the streets drunkenly, arms flung over shoulders, calling obscenely to passing women. The wharves reeked of fish and salt, and nights were smudged with lamp soot and weak yellow light. Every time he met another sailor, he'd be told once again where the best brothels were. "Nickel a throw," they'd say, unashamed. "Get yourself a dollar's worth." Rulon prayed and prayed, and remembered the exhortations of the brethren — their appeals to chastity and purity, their warning of the Lord's watchfulness over everything.

Lust tore at him. He couldn't stop thinking about what it would be like. Finally he went to the address in Chinatown. The woman had light brown hair that smelled of chemicals and flowers, and her lips tasted waxy. Afterward, Rulon was not quite sure what had happened between them — could not picture the way their bodies had come together. He knew only the surge of intensity that wrapped his hips and shot up his spine. "Already?" the woman said in a teasing voice, and Rulon opened his eyes and noticed she was much younger than she had at first appeared, the skin around her eyes smooth and unwrinkled, the pores on her nose tiny.

Her scent haunted him, back to his hotel and through the night, and as he thought of her I thought of faithless Sally Bartram, my fiancée, whom I had never kissed, who had smiled with half-closed eyes as we'd danced at the ward house on Friday nights, her hand light on my shoulder. I remembered how I was choked with the desire to press into her, *through* her, and I wanted Rulon to go back now, to return again and again.

For two days he prayed inside his room. He told himself he must have passed through the war and into hell. The city was never quiet, and the lights burned all night. The third day, he went back and spent a dime. He told himself it didn't matter whether he committed this sin, because he'd done worse, but he felt watched and ashamed as he walked the narrow streets and went up the stairs to the door marked by a sign in Chinese characters. In the front room, men sat on couches, murmuring with the girls. Sheer red cloth draped the lamps, shading the room in crimson. Rulon asked for the woman by name: *Irene.* Walking home, he could smell her perfume, now familiar, and taste her smoky breath, and he knew he had stained his soul. He left for home the following day, and he could not stop thinking of Irene, of her cheap stockings draped over a bedpost, the thrill of her carnal smile, the fleshy rub of her belly against his.

He rode the train first to Boise and then to Pocatello, where his folks waited for him at the train platform. His father's beard seemed longer, spreading like an apron below his collarbone. He wore simple wool clothing, threadbare gray pants hemmed high above the ankles of his boots. His mother—my niece, a girl I had barely known now grown into a woman who carried weariness in her frame—wore a gingham dress, made from a pattern of pale blue with tiny flowers. They took a room in a hotel—Rulon on the floor and his parents in the small bed—and then caught the one daily train to Franklin the next morning. Rulon watched the landscape as the train lurched and smoked, the tan floor of the desert spotted with dusty sage.

Rulon settled at the farm and worked with his father. Spreading across the wide valley floor to the east of the town, the Warren place was one of the biggest in the county, a range of wheat and barley and cattle pasture that Rulon's father had expanded year after year. In the center sat the magisterial two-storied house, painted white, with a steeply pitched roof and a row of box elders on the west side. A grid of ditches and culverts, hand dug, lined the fields, and Rulon's father was often consulted by the other men in town about irrigation and farm practices. Rulon's older sister had married while he was still in school; she lived four miles away on a smaller farm, on the other side of town, with her husband and children. When Rulon returned, the planting was done and everything was greening, the land fresh and bristly under the warm sun. Rulon loved getting out into the fields and emptying his mind, carrying a shovel along the ditch bank or hauling hay to the cattle.

He didn't know what he would do and didn't wonder. He wanted only cool mornings in an empty room as the first line of sunlight traced the horizon, hot afternoons on a dusty ditch berm, cool evenings with the moon white in the window. Empty rooms and dreaming. Empty rooms and the remembered feel of sheer stockings, the taste of lipstick, the motion of Irene's head on the pillow, her mocking little laugh. He could no longer picture her face, but could envision the skin under her eyes and along her nose, could remember the moment he realized how young she was — seventeen? sixteen? younger? He eyed the girls in church now and felt intense impurity. He could make a whole life out of doing that, pants folded over a chair, an hour's rest and back at it. Sin was sin, and how much could it compound? He had already broken a commandment many times over: Thou shalt not kill. All those Germans. That, plus three times with

Irene and, more appalling, his delight in it, his continued delight. How could his eternal reward be worse now if he abandoned himself to a life of murder and fornication? And yet he could not. He yearned for sin, and then forgiveness, and then for sin, and he could not decide, moment to moment, where the wickedness was greater: in himself, in the church, or in the world.

I wanted to tell him they were only Huns. Pile them up. I would have fired those guns myself and laughed as the Germans sank. I wanted to tell him he was but a man upon the earth. But I could not influence him, could not make my presence real in any way. Sometimes I concentrated thoughts and tried to send them to him, tried to wish him into acting. *Close it now,* I would think, as he read from the Book of Mormon during church. *Close it.* I tried to focus my command into a beam of light. *Close it, Rulon. It is folly.* I was desperate for him to hear me. What was my existence otherwise? I tried and tried to make a ripple in the world. To be there.

Rulon's parents invited Ann Lawton to dinner without telling him. She arrived one Sunday after church, in a new-looking dress of pale blue that hung so low it covered her feet and rose snugly to her neck and traveled down to her wrists. She was seventeen, the bishop's daughter, quietly bold. She wore her long brown hair in a single braid and was delicate but for her chapped red ears. Her father was the bishop who had blessed Rulon when he shipped out, the one who had reassured him, and he felt false before both father and daughter.

After church that Sunday, before Ann arrived, Rulon had gone to his room, up the narrow stairs and at the end of a dim hall. He had taken off his tie and dress shoes and lain on his bed, watching the play of light on the wall as the curtain lifted and fell before the open window. An eddy in time arrived, and he entered it. He drifted near sleep. His legs and hips lightened, as though they were lifting with the curtain, and his head became warm and damp, and the sound of his breath lulled him, until his mother called.

Going downstairs in his stocking feet, he heard his mother say, "Rulon, come say hello to Ann." He stopped. He was aware that from the living room below, where his family and their guest sat waiting for him, his feet and the legs of his trousers were visible. The room was bright with sunlight, and he could hear his nieces and nephews clattering about on the porch. Resentment filled his mind. He had gone to sea and done what he had done, and now was being denied peace, the only thing he sought. His fury covered all the people he knew, all the people who continued to live, to eat Sunday dinner and hang clothing on the line and take baths in fresh water and have picnics and parades and ask smiling questions about the war. Sometimes at church he imagined the heads of the Saints exploding silently — the bishop's head as he stood at the pulpit, the heads of the men who sidled up to him, the heads of the people in the pew in front

of him, one by one in time with the hymns, a wave of magi-
cal death bursting amid the empty talk of sin. Now he imagined it happening with his family, a popping sound repeated
throughout the house — his mother in the living room, sister in the kitchen, her husband on the porch with his father,
leaving his nieces and nephews out of it — the bodies strewn
about while he slept the silent day away. I experienced it,
too — the throb of adrenaline and anger, flooding me just
as it had in the days before my death — and I could not begrudge him.

At dinner, though, Rulon was fine. He talked to Ann about
the crops and teased her about boys in the ward. His parents and sister mostly listened to them talk, joining in when
there was a pause, pressing them along. They passed the
large crockery bowls filled with potatoes and beans again
and again. Rulon looked at Ann and saw Irene, and beneath
the table he swelled. He felt guilty for besmirching Ann with
his thoughts, and yet he didn't try to stop. He imagined her
bare shoulder blades, placing a freckle on the right one. He
imagined the dip in her collarbone, pink nipples, pale belly, a
wild thicket of hair. He imagined her embarrassed whispers.
Rulon could not tell, but I could see in the speckled flush
that bloomed on Ann's neck and face when they talked, and
in the way her eyes darted away from his, that she had already decided she loved him.

After dinner, Rulon walked her down the dirt lane to her
house, his irritation having vanished in the easy pleasure
of her company. A ditch ran alongside the lane, and insects

spun above the thick green grass, catching the coppery afternoon light. I thought: *Take her hand.* She told him of the scandals from the ward dances: which girls disappeared and returned with which boys. She told him the gossip about Brother Lundeblad drinking whiskey, how his sons had to keep the farm going. His hands swung loose at his sides. *Take her hand, Rulon. Turn her toward you.* When they reached her house, she reached for his hand while he said good-bye, and it froze his words. Back in his room, he tugged at himself furiously, thinking first of Irene and then of Ann, and fell to his bed in shame.

I was with him then, as in all moments. There was nothing in Rulon's mind that made me sorry for his soul. *Do not be ashamed.* I imagined my voice, rich with the cadenced tones of a prophet. *You are but a man upon the earth. You are forgiven.* I watched and I wondered again about my own existence. *You will need no forgiveness.* I had been with him for eighteen months now, but no part of me could reach him. He brooded over every little sin. I dreaded the idea that this was all of life left to me, and that it might plod on and on. I wanted to press against Rulon, to force him into action. Any action. *There is no forgiveness you will ever need.*

For weeks, Rulon did little but work on the farm, irrigating the fields, clearing weeds from the ditches. The wheat turned golden, the heads of barley grew heavy, and the warm afternoon breezes made waves of the fields. His parents suggested daily that he walk up the lane to the Lawtons, that he pay Ann a visit, that he sit beside her at church. But he could not. When he was with Ann, he would turn her into Irene. It became impossible to sit comfortably with her. He was convinced his lust was apparent to all. He spoke less and less. Sometimes when his mother asked him a question, he walked away without answering, or merely kept his eyes on his plate. He could not marry Ann Lawton, nor any other righteous woman, for he no longer desired their righteousness. And yet he could not stop thinking of Ann. At church, she looked for him when he came in, and despite himself he would smile or nod. He felt his every glance was a lie, and he should no longer live around people.

When he learned that the government was going to open a post office in Franklin, he applied for the position. He got the job — mostly, he was told by the visiting postmaster from Pocatello, because he was a war hero — and decided to move into a room in the back of the new pine-smelling post office they had built on the town's main street.

The news shocked Rulon's parents. Though he would be in town, just three miles away, it was a larger departure than they had ever expected. He was their only son. His mother wept, and his father told him the farm would be there for him when he got tired of the post office.

"I always figured you'd take this place over," his father said. They were sitting in the living room before supper. Fall was coming, twilight sifting down earlier each day. Soon harvest would begin.

"I'll help you get the wheat and barley put up, and then go," Rulon said. "I'm not sure it was ever really for me."

His parents were confused, I could tell, because it was a lie. Rulon took naturally to farm work, walking the fields and testing the moisture of the soil, checking for stripe rust on the wheat, calming cows to put medicine drops into their great glassy eyes. But Rulon wanted silence at meals. Freedom in the afternoons. He wanted never to discuss the war again with any smiling face, never to sit across a family table laden with bread and jam and roasted meat and pretend chastity with any woman.

Go, I thought. *Go*. I wanted something new. I had followed his dreary routine, day upon day, and sensed his desperate faith, his clutching need to be righteous, and I sometimes thought this was a hell after all, one that revealed itself slowly. A hell of Rulon's making, which could end only when he did.

Rulon rode into town together with his father. He was calm as the wagon clattered along, and was grateful his father didn't speak. I sensed the moment was right for me then. *Rulon*. If my existence was all there was to eternity, why should he be deviled by sin, by guilt, by propriety? Why should he not live a life of happy moments? *Follow your will.* I could not fathom my existence. Were there others like me? Out there among the living, behind their eyes? The days were pale, emptied of meaning. *Follow your will.* I wanted Rulon to burn down the tedium of my days. But he was like a branch floating downriver, and I was a leaf fallen beside him, drifting without weight on the water.

II

Rulon loved the post office and his simple little room in back: his bed, a small table and one chair, his navy trunk, and a couple of shelves. His belongings had fit neatly in four boxes. On the shelves were his Book of Mormon and a few novels his mother had used as a schoolteacher, before she married: *Great Expectations, The Scarlet Letter, Les Misérables*. And the notebooks in which he had begun keeping a journal, pages filled with the turmoil of his mind.

In this room, he wrote, *with this one candle flame, the wind in the darkness, I can believe that I am alone upon the earth, perfectly, peacefully alone. Here is where I can worship. Here is where I can feel the Lord's spirit. Here, not in the lukewarm clamor and stink of the ward house, where everywhere you look is compromise and cowardice.*

The mail arrived every afternoon, a gray canvas bag that shuffled with secrets. Rulon welcomed it with a kind of reverence, and he handed over the outgoing sack with the same solemnity — the same reserve that animated his actions when he took the sacrament on Sundays, the gentle way he held the trays, the tiny cups of water, the bits of torn bread. The body and the blood. The sacrament had become real for him. He had held bits of flesh and bone between his fingers, just as he held the bread now, and when he tasted the bread he believed he was tasting the living flesh of Christ, and some days he believed it saved him, and some days he believed there was not enough holy flesh in all the world to erase his wickedness.

Winter came hard. It snowed in mid-October and stayed cold for weeks, solidifying the coarse snow. Rulon wore all his clothes and burned wood in his stove, but the wind slipped through the walls of the post office and chased away the heat.

Each day, Rulon sorted the letters into PO Boxes and waited on customers and filled the gray sacks to go back to Pocatello and beyond. He enjoyed the order and predictability of the work and missed the open space and days of the farm less than he had imagined he would. His parents stopped by more than they needed to, and he always greeted them formally, like a servant, until his mother, baffled and hurt, stopped coming altogether.

His father kept at it, quietly. "OK, son," he would say, taking his mail and preparing to leave. "I know your mother would like to see you sometime. You could come for supper on Sunday."

"Sunday would not be possible," Rulon said, flipping through a handful of envelopes.

"Some other day, then."

Rulon didn't answer, though it made him sad to keep silent. His father left, a wintry gust banging into the room. Rulon could not explain what had happened inside him, but he did not want to be with others.

He riffled the envelopes in his hand again. Rulon loved handling the mail, the thick brown envelopes and the smudged white ones, the letters and the packages, stamped red and blue, the announcement of all the world outside of Franklin. He paid attention to who got what. Families got a lot of letters from Salt Lake. The Johansens got a letter a week from North Dakota; the Popes two a week from Nauvoo, Illinois. Frank Staley got special orders for fabric and dry goods from wholesalers in San Francisco or Minneapolis. One day Rulon saw a letter for Ann Lawton, posted in Chicago, from "Elder Britton." Two weeks later, he saw another. Jake Britton, a kid Rulon used to torment at ward picnics and youth nights. On a mission in Chicago and writing letters home to Ann. Like most returning veterans, Rulon hadn't served a mission, but most other young men did, two years spent trying to bring far-flung people into the fold.

Rulon had told himself he was finished with Ann, but when he saw the third letter from Elder Britton he slid it into the front pocket of his apron. Later he burned it at his table, wrote three angry pages in his journal about the spiritual weakness of the young, consumed as they were by lust and worldly emotions, and was then embarrassed before himself for his hypocrisy.

I came to hate the post office for just what Rulon loved — its tedious repetition, the sanctuary of routine. It was not so different from the plodding days on the farm. His days were my days, and I yearned for them to pulse with blood, with lust. *Go see Ann.* I'd send the futile messages. *Go to her.* Sometimes I thought Rulon was weakening and we were floating toward each other. As he sat in sacrament meeting, seething at the bishop's milky tones, I'd think: *Challenge him, Rulon. Denounce him.* He wanted peace, and I daydreamed of his violent end. It had been so thrilling to die. *Scatter their letters, Rulon. Make a fire in the night.*

In the early evenings, after work and before he settled into his reading and writing, Rulon walked outside of town, along the fields — places that reminded me of my life. Once he stood on a ditch bank east of town, watching the gold and purple light on the Tetons and the gentle apron of hills easing into the valley. It called me to a specific moment from my own life — an exact replay of the light on the mountainside, the melancholy beauty of the dusk, the comforting silence that follows a day of noise and effort. I was walking home from Brother Miller's farm after an afternoon of putting up hay, flush with exhaustion. The memory brought back a keen surge of love for my physical self. How I missed my body! I missed swinging my arms and scratching my neck. I missed the sensation of meat and milk in my mouth, the crust of drool on my cheek upon waking.

I thought of my father, reading from the Book of Mormon at the family table, interpreting it for the rest of us. "There shall be opposition in all things," I could hear him say, in his whispery baritone. "Without darkness there can be no light. Without weakness, no strength. Without evil, no good."

I was waiting along with Rulon for an opposing force, for

something to press against. Something in this world, some person or idea, was the opposite of me, and I needed to crash into it to become whoever or whatever I was.

Every morning, Rulon rose before dawn and read from his Book of Mormon or from Revelation. He was hounded by guilt over the war, over the iron-handed lust that seized him at night, and he repented daily. But he also became more concerned with the sins of others, and he sometimes felt righteous by comparison. He saw the end days all around him and believed he was surrounded by corruption and hypocrisy. He came to think that, through the war, the community was built on a foundation of killing, contracted and paid for, to be done quietly and beyond the curtain of the everyday.

In his journal: *Today, a parade in Richmond for three returning seamen. A murderer's parade. The brethren there wanted me to greet the men, welcome them back, form friendships, etc. They came to me to ask it, and I told them I could not.*

Rulon started missing church. The only reason he'd been going at all was guilt over his mother — she seemed drawn and shocked all the time now, as though she had never imagined anything as bad as this estrangement.

Again, in his journal: *The Church has become the Whore of Babylon, calling forth the last days. It has strayed from the hard path of righteousness. It loves comfort and compliance, and respects no suffering but submission.*

I, too, had broken with the Church, had cried out for a

more vigorous gospel. Now I didn't care about any of that. *Hear me, Rulon. Heed me.* I didn't care what Rulon believed or what the bishop believed or what the people in the ward believed, because I knew they were wrong. *Make a fire in the night.* None of their hells described my hell. I did not understand what was happening to me, but I knew — with a faith surpassing any I'd ever had — that it had all been false, everything I had believed, it had all been a fantasy or a joke, and this imitation of life was all I would ever have. Sometimes I hated Rulon, hated his weakness with Ann, hated the dull and pointless struggle in his soul. *Listen.* I prayed to him at all hours, not without hope that he might one day answer. *Listen, brother. Listen.* I craved his death, to find whether I would perish with him or live on.

One night as Rulon slept, he dreamed he was in a field in spring, holding the smooth wooden handles of the plow and standing behind the sagging rump of the family mule. A fog of dust surrounded him. Shapes floated into clarity before his face. He saw his shipmate from the *Gooding,* a plug of tobacco in his cheek, saying with a wink and a leer, "You look at her right, sailor, and her drawers fall to the floor." His father floated forward and said, "Nephi said barley out back and potatoes here." His sister, saying, "Ann Lawton, Ann Lawton." Then a face he didn't recognize, the pinched, unhappy countenance of a woman, hair pulled into a bun behind her head. "John Wilder," she said, "your father paid a dime to have that sharpened."

The words rushed to me across time, as clearly as sound over water. The woman was my mother, exact in every way, and the moment returned to me: I was eight years old, and due to some misdeed was hiding from my father in the firewood lean-to behind the house. After a while, when it became clear my father wasn't coming after me, I took up his ax and walked around the dirt yard, chipping it gently against the cross posts in the fence and on the rocky ground.

I hadn't tried to send Rulon the dream. He had drawn it from me somehow. Or I had melted into him. I tried even harder then to send him my thoughts, often the simplest things — *Take one more bite of beans. Now another. Now the bread.* Sometimes he would do as I said. *Open the letter.* Was it coincidence? Every life needs its faith. I longed for a voice. A prophet's voice. A patriarch's. If Rulon ever heard me, he might think it was the voice of the Lord.

Soon after the dream, Rulon attended sacrament meeting for the last time. He listened to Bishop Lawton's placating tones, his soft calls to righteousness. He watched the back of Ann Lawton's head, the stray strands of hair that caught the light and burned as golden filaments, and he could not chase away the lust. *Go to her. Find a way.*

That night he slipped into sleep and awoke inside a dream, a vision of Franklin and the surrounding valley from a rocky promontory in the Tetons. It looked like a view from heaven, from some impossibly high place. A voice spoke in words of an unknown language, and when Rulon turned, he looked upon a face that I knew well.

The man was Orin Jensen. As Rulon floated toward him, Orin spoke, calling him by my name. "They are coming, Brother Wilder. Our moment is nigh."

Rulon was dreaming my life, dreaming my last days on earth.

We had fled into the mountains — Orin, myself, and five others. The Idaho territory had passed the Test-Oath Act, banning Mormons from voting or holding office. This, after some counties had thrown good Mormon men in jail for celestial marriage and fired Mormon teachers. When the bishop called on the Saints to obey that law, to refrain from voting, I knew my break with the Church had come.

"Render to Caesar the things that are Caesar's," the bishop said, in his ignorance and weakness.

Orin organized the resistance — we would render nothing to Caesar. We would formally renounce the Church and go to the polls, where we could honestly present ourselves as non-Mormons. Afterward, we would rebaptize one another into a new church with a new mission. A true church, which would not bow and truckle. When we arrived at the polls in Pocatello, a mob stood already in the street. They held signs with vile slogans and shouted as we tried to make our way inside. I blazed with hatred for those faces, the black pits of their eyes, their rotten mouths. We had settled this land — Mormons had, our families had. We should have been the ones guarding the polls and turning away the wicked.

Our plan failed. We were well-known as the faithful. Despite our claims, the deputies tried to arrest us for voter fraud, and we fled into the mountains. After our first night, Orin led us down to the valley, where we killed and half skinned a calf on the ranch of one of the town marshals, carving off as much as we could haul back. They might have left us alone if not for that, but peace was not what we wanted.

In Rulon's dream he watched — and I watched, watched and remembered — as the posse came slowly up a field of shale toward our position behind a ledge. It was just as it was then, everything just as it was. I rested the sights of my rifle on the brown hat of the posse's leader. The rifleshot cracked and echoed through the mountains. The man fell. A ruby shadow grew from his head on the shale.

Orin floated into Rulon's view. "Now you know," he said. "Now you know." And Rulon awoke, certain he had been sent a vision from the Lord. He spent the night praying for guidance. I thought: *Do not pray, brother. Act.* I wanted to be the answer to his prayers. I wanted him to know the joy of my final days, the joy that came from the force of our opposition. I wanted to live it again. *Act, Rulon.* After I shot that man, we spent two weeks in the mountains, the nights so cold we clung to one another for warmth. The first posse had been coming to arrest us; we knew the next one would not be so docile. During the days, Orin preached to us a new gospel of righteous resistance — calling for the homeland and for the faithful that we had come west to establish — and we burned with it. We rebaptized each other one day in an icy stream.

This was a holy war, Orin said. I never sorrowed for killing that man, and yet I feared the only atonement would come through blood — my blood spilled upon the earth. But Orin said there was no need for the blood sacrifice.

"Scripture tells us, Brother Wilder, that it is the murderer whose blood must spill. The warrior will live forever in God's light."

I was unconvinced. One night, I slipped away and knelt beneath a pine tree. I prayed to the Lord to forgive me, and I pricked my finger and squeezed three drops of blood onto the ground. They formed tiny black beads in the moonlight, and I knew how paltry I was before the Lord, because I was not remorseful in my heart.

The sheriff's men returned, with a bigger posse. They swarmed us from all sides and made no attempt at capture. Before I felt the blade in my ribs, I saw a man open Orin's throat with the slash of a knife. A horrific red gape appeared and rained down his chest. Lying on the ground, I watched my own blood pool on the soft earth, creeping among the pine needles and stones, a true atonement at last, and I slept in the certainty of my salvation, rushing, rushing toward the celestial kingdom, my eternal reward.

Rulon opened the next letter from Elder Britton, who wrote of his disappointment at not having a letter from Ann for two weeks.

Rulon studied the close, tiny handwriting. Much of the letter was simply news of Britton's life — he was serving in Chicago, working in the urban neighborhoods, "baptizing few." Rulon wondered how far it had gone between Britton and Ann. It had been months since he had last walked the lane with Ann. He slid Britton's letter between the pages of his Book of Mormon.

Ann came to the post office three days after the letter had arrived. It was March; a smell of chill air and water lay under everything and rushed into the room with her. Rulon sorted letters behind the counter, and when she entered, his face flushed, tightening around the eyes. He feared his voice would tremble and show everything about him.

"Hello, Rule," she said.

"Hello, Miss Lawton," he said with mock formality, but the words were awkward in his mouth. "I'm glad to see you."

"I'm surprised to hear you say it."

She smiled thinly, holding something back. Rulon's heart boomed in his ears, and I heard it too, thinking, *Take her, take her,* his lust my own, instantaneous, everywhere.

Ann said, "I might have thought you hadn't taken any notice one way or the other. Shut up in here all day." As usual, her dress was buttoned to the neck and covered her to her ankles and wrists, but for Rulon the room was suffused with the warm breath of her flesh, damp and eager.

"You know better," he said, and, after a pause, added quickly, "There's no mail for you."

"There's a dance Saturday at the ward house."

"I heard that."

Ann went crimson to her hairline, turned, and left.

Fluttering light filled Rulon. It was only 4:20 p.m., but he pulled the shade on the door and hung the CLOSED sign and went back to his room. He retrieved the letter from Britton to Ann and read it again. He took out his notebook and pen, smoothed Britton's letter beside it, and began to write a new letter in close, tiny handwriting like Britton's own.

He copied the first paragraph exactly. And some of the next ones, too. Then he wrote: *I heard of the fire at the ward dance from Jenny Monson. Jenny writes me fairly regular. She is a funny girl that I love to hear from and one who can tell a good story. Her letters don't hold a candle to yours, Ann, but they are entertaining.*

He tucked the letter into an envelope, copied the address, stamped the envelope, and put it in the box labeled Lawton.

Rulon went to the dance Saturday. He stood along the wall near the door and watched as the dancers moved in and out of the lantern light. He hated every laughing face. He dreamed of their glorious deaths. Then he saw Ann, serving drinks and popcorn balls at the folding tables, and his anger ebbed. She looked at him, tipped her head toward the dance floor, and smiled. Rulon blushed. He walked to her and of-fered his arm, and they joined the next dance. He was a ter-rible dancer, but he stomped through the steps with vigor. Ann smiled at him and laughed often. A couple of times, as she turned past him, he smelled talcum and cream, and he knew that it rose from under her clothes, and lust inflamed him. Coming off the dance floor, he ran into his mother and father, standing awkwardly to the side as though they were not waiting for him. Seeing them, he felt caught, and

he could barely bring himself to speak. His father asked formal questions about the PO, and his mother asked him what
he was eating, desperately trying to sound casual, and she
laughed once, a shrill, false note. They parted after a long
pause, like strangers forced together at a funeral.

Later, in his bed, he imagined Ann coming to him, em-
boldened, roughened, remade as Irene, red lips opening on
teeth of pearl gray, breathing a stream of forbidden cigarette
smoke through her pursed lips into the night air, lowering
herself onto him, hair hanging in his face, talking to him all
the while, talking in Irene's throaty voice, talking.

Ann wrote back to Britton. Hurt and reserve lay under every word, though she didn't mention Jenny Monson. Rulon
took out a sheet of paper and wrote his own letter to Britton,
carefully, in Ann's handwriting, saying she'd met someone
new: *I have become closer to this man than I intended, and
now I feel it would be dishonest of me to say otherwise. I feel I
owe you that, you've been such a dear friend to me.*

They were the words Sally Bartram had written to me in
1865, mere weeks after she had moved with her family to
Salt Lake City. Faithless Sally Bartram. When I saw those
words come from Rulon's hand — "such a dear friend" — I remembered the moment I had first read them, on our porch,
an autumn day, in the heat of the afternoon, and I remembered my mother coming out while I read.

Rulon sealed the letter and mailed it to Elder Britton.

He began opening other letters. Sometimes he wrote replies. He wrote to one family that their sister in Nebraska had died of smallpox, the day after everyone thought the fever had broken.

It was the precise manner of my mother's death.

He wrote a letter denying an extension on a loan payment to Roy Kalper, the largest landowner in the county. The words he used were the very words I had written — over and over again — as a clerk in my uncle's bank in Minneapolis, when my parents sent me to stay with him the summer of 1858.

Rulon believed he was inventing the stories, that he was being inspired to sow chaos in these placid lives. They would learn the truth eventually, he thought, and their sorrow would not last. But a nervous sliver would be left in their hearts, and he knew that they would trace the letters back to him eventually, and he wanted that. I wanted it, too, whatever it meant for Rulon.

Several weeks after he forged the letter to Elder Britton from Ann, she stopped at the post office on a Sunday afternoon. Rulon was lying on his cot, reading a Natty Bumppo novel. He read for hours every day now, Scripture and novels borrowed from the little "library" shelf set up at the store, and he began to consider the idea of writing something more himself, something more than journal entries or the tales he was spinning in the letters. An accounting. A testament.

Ann knocked and said his name quietly, and he sat up on his cot, silent for nearly a minute before deciding to open the door. The sun was behind her, throwing her face into shadow, ringed by a corona of light. She held a basket with a cloth folded over the top.

"Hello, Rule," she said, smiling.

I pitied her then, to be chasing him so. She was losing her pride. But Rulon's desire flared, and it raised in me again how I missed my human form.

"What are you smuggling in that basket?" Rulon asked, and he was thrilled at his easy tone, his clerk's glibness. "Come in so I can get a look."

She had brought him cinnamon rolls, and they shared one at his little table. He sat on the bed, and she used the chair. No one else had been inside the room. As they ate, Rulon realized with a start how shoddy it looked, as though he were waking up to something he had ceased to see. His thread-worn clothing sat in a pile on his trunk. Sheets of paper, covered with scrawls, were scattered about. Pieces of mail lay on the floor, on the bed, on the little shelf. A package to the dry-goods store sat in the corner, unopened. It occurred to him, too late, that he ought to have hidden the mail before he invited Ann in. She noticed it, and uncertainty entered her attitude.

He told her he had been reading in the Book of Mormon and praying about it; he didn't want his absence at church to give her the idea that he was losing his righteousness. I wanted him to put that aside. I was remembering Irene and thinking that Rulon could simply take Ann. Overpower her. *Embrace her.* He struggled to explain himself to Ann. He could not tell her how he had become convinced the Lord was warning him away from the Church, because her father was the bishop and because it was the foundation of her entire life. It would only sound like wickedness to her.

Finally she said she had to leave. *Kiss her. Take her skirt in your fists.* Rulon stood beside her as she wrapped the rolls and put the empty basket on her arm, and he looked down at the fine hairs on the back of her neck, the final flesh before her blue dress rose and covered her. He reached out his hand but did not know how to begin. *Seize her.* He placed his right arm around her shoulder abruptly and buried his face in her neck, sensed the warmth of her skin. *Kiss her on the mouth.* He pressed his lips to her neck, feeling she might turn to him, but she stiffened and remained rigid. Her silence told him the depth of his mistake. She simply waited, playing dead, then left when he released her, not once raising her head. Rulon sat on his bed for hours, as it grew darker and darker.

I whispered to him all through that night. *Scatter the letters. Make a fire in the night.* I could feel his shame, his conviction that he did not belong among people. Was there room for me inside him now? *Be a force against. A force opposed.* And the rushing flume of his anger, growing out of all of it, washed us closer and closer together.

III

Rulon didn't open the PO the next day. He stayed in the back as people came and knocked, shouted for him, and then left him to silence. He emerged only when he heard the mail wagon, in the afternoon. After collecting the canvas bag silently from Broom Janson, he turned back toward his room.

Rulon dumped the contents of the bag on his bed. Something about it nauseated him. *Burn it.* A network of human connections, built on lies and comfort. He picked up the first letter and tore it open. News of the Nebraska prairie to Glenda McDevit from a niece. He opened another. A report from a missionary to his parents. Another. A bill for milk delivery. *Burn it.* He opened every envelope and package, and when he was finished he stuffed it all back into the canvas sack and lifted it over his shoulder. *Burn them all.* He went out and walked to the middle of the street, the short, graded dirt road that ran between the five buildings of downtown Franklin — the dry goods store, the PO, the ward house, the livery, and the tiny jailhouse. Rulon emptied the sack in the street and kicked the torn pieces of mail as though they were autumn leaves. It was a weekday afternoon and the street was not busy, but the few people there stopped what they were doing and stared at him.

We were moving, the two of us, and gaining speed.

Sister Bingham came out of the dry goods store, and behind her, Brother Barry, the store's owner. They squinted against the lowering sun at Rulon, as though he presented an enduring mystery.

"Greetings, Sister Bingham! Brother Barry!" Rulon waved in an exaggerated manner. He was filled with the Lord's pulsing light, and would not have been surprised to find himself rising above the earth. He laughed. "See you in church on Sunday!"

He marched back to the PO. For the first time, he found the room uncomfortable. The space leaned against him. He imagined they were out there, everyone, the whole town. He pulled the curtains on his little window.

No one came to his door. He heard them outside in the hour after he had dumped the mail, heard voices and confused laughter, heard the patient tones the brethren applied to him, knew the patronizing manner in which they were speaking of him. He prayed at his bedside, on his knees, hands clasped together so firmly his knuckles ached, and he asked the Lord how he should begin.

He didn't open the post office the next day, either, and no one knocked. He sensed the town's knowledge surrounding him but could not imagine what they might do. He heard the mail wagon pull up in the afternoon, and he rushed out once again to greet it.

"Good afternoon, Doctor Warren," Broom said jovially. This was one of his standard jokes — to call people "Doctor." "Here's some more of your medicine."

Rulon despised Broom, despised his nonsense and his happiness. He lifted the canvas sack from the back of the wagon and looked up at Broom, sitting on the buckboard seat. *Knock him from that seat.*

"Shut your ridiculous mouth," he told Broom quietly, and

turned back toward his room. As he reached the door to his room, he heard Broom mutter, "All right," and then the brief slap of the reins before the wagon rattled into motion.

A few minutes later, when he could no longer hear Broom's wagon wheels outside, he reemerged with the bag over one shoulder and his kerosene lamp in the other hand. I stayed silent. I knew. Rulon heard his blood in his ears. He dumped the sack on the same spot he had the day before. The street was silent. A young woman and a child watched him from down the street, and a curtain peeled back in the upstairs window of the store before falling back into place. He held the burning wick to the corner of one letter, and then another. Soon the pile curled and blackened, wavering in the flames of gold and orange, and it was beautiful.

Deputations came and went from Rulon's door for three days, and he stayed in his room, lying on the cot, eating hard biscuits and dried meat, while they knocked and demanded and left. Bishop Lawton came twice, and Verl Gentling, the part-time sheriff, three times.

The mail stopped arriving. Soon someone would break down the door.

Rulon tried to imagine what he would do. He thought about leaving everything behind. He believed the Lord was calling him to a radical act, and I wanted him to answer — to something, to whatever. *You are outside them. You are their enemy.* I was sick of his prayers, of his constant yearning for God, but he wanted to die a righteous death, and in this, we were one. I wanted that thrill once more. And then I wanted him gone, to see what shape my existence would take.

In his room, he felt adrift on a raft, floating ever farther from the ship. He thought the ship might no longer be visible. Sometimes he stayed on his cot for hours, imagining he was surrounded by water and safe only there. Sometimes he imagined he was underground, burrowed into the earth, and no one could reach him.

On the third night after he had burned the mail, Rulon left his room after midnight. He stood in the street and peered at the town; the April night was cool, freshening him like water. He started walking toward his family's house.

Make a fire in the night.

The night sky was blue and the land black, and a bright curve of moon reclined above the mountains to the east. Rulon followed the dirt road toward the mountains, whose night shade hid the homes that spread outward from town. As he walked he remembered the gunner's mate from the ship, Sawicki, a Pole from Chicago who talked like no one Rulon had ever met, who told vile stories about women and swore more than any other sailor on board, and still prayed each night, holding a necklace with a cross in his hands as his lips made their silent ministrations. On the day of the battle with the *Gotthilf,* in the North Sea, Rulon had been navigating, working the wheel that spun the big gun. Sawicki was the gunner, and his head had vanished almost in silence, everything around them so loud. The nose of the gun slumped forward, and Sawicki collapsed onto the deck. Another gunner took over, and it was three hours later when Rulon realized that he had been covered in a spray of sticky pink and slivers of bone. He picked a bit of something from his shoulder and what he saw there, pinched between his fingers, took in the whole human world: a fragment of bone, three black hairs, a red-black clump.

He came to the crossroads now and turned south, toward his family's home. The more he walked, the brighter the night seemed, though there was scarce light from the crescent moon. Rulon's spirit vibrated at a perfect pitch between calm and discord. It seemed natural to me, like I was sliding alongside him in a groove.

The war seemed long ago to Rulon, and he was surprised at the heat and energy that accompanied his memories. Whatever he might do now, he thought, he was justified. He remembered the Germans in the ocean. He imagined what it must have been like for them in the icy water, desperate to live and waving their arms in surrender, begging to be spared only to feel the metal burn of the bullets. Now he knew what he should have done: He should have defended the Germans. He should have stopped his fellow sailors, attacked them. He should have acted as a lone, righteous soul.

I thought he was foolish to care so much — still, after all this time. But I loved what was happening inside him, as if his mind was reaching for mine.

Act, Rulon. Act.

When he reached his parents' house, he went to the shed and selected an ax, a heavy one with a sharp, gleaming blade, and he walked to the house and went quietly in the front door. He stood in the entryway and listened, and hearing only his own galloping blood, he stepped to the closet under the stairs and lifted his father's rifle and a box of shells from the top shelf.

Be a force against.

He went outside to the barn, where he harnessed his father's mule and led him out to the road, and then back toward town. As he walked, I sent him thoughts in an unending stream. I imagined them as commands.

Be a force against. An opponent. Make a fire in the night. Act, Rulon. By your actions will you prove your righteousness. Act. Act. That word, like a mantra.

He stopped abruptly, in the middle of the road, and whispered angrily: "I *am* acting. I *am*."

His words came into me like a hot blade. Like a beautiful wound that tells you you're alive.

You are my brother, Rulon. You will follow me into eternity.

But there was only silence after that. Silence and the sound of his steps in the pale night.

At the PO, Rulon took his trunk and packed it with his bedroll, his notebooks, his Book of Mormon, a sack of beans and a piece of pork fat, extra pants and shirt. He strapped it onto the back of the mule and returned to the rear of the PO, where he had leaned the rifle and the ax. He picked up the ax and held it with both hands. It felt like an instrument of balance. *Make a fire.* He carried the ax to the front office, lit a kerosene lamp, and stood before the PO boxes, the rows and columns of square holes, the names of the townspeople listed below: Jansen, Bingham, Lawton, Strengel, Pope, Miller, Warren. The boxes made a grid, and Rulon's first swing buried the ax with a splintering crack in its exact middle. His second swing sent a burst of wood careening past his head, and his third brought four boxes off the wall completely. He swung again and again until the boxes lay in splinters at his feet, and then he turned the ax on the desk and the partition where people came for their mail, and on the tables where he sorted it and then on the floors themselves, the planking, and then the walls, the door, the windows with a glassy shatter. *Bring it down.* By the time he rested, he had turned it all back to simple wood, piles of fuel. The night shone through gaps in the walls where he had driven the ax through. *Make a fire.* I thought then that Rulon wanted to do it, to burn it all, but he saw the chaos he had made and he changed his mind. He wanted to leave it as a monument. In this he was right. I wanted it then, too. He took the ax and rifle and mounted his father's mule. The street was silent, and no lights appeared in the windows of the nearest houses well down the lane. He began riding slowly into the desert.

As the mule swayed under him, Rulon sank into warm weariness. He wondered how long it would take the brethren to come for him. Then, for the first time, it occurred to him that they might not follow.

They might forgive him.

This was not what he wanted. He wanted them to come

for him, and I wanted them to come for him, to come relentlessly, so many he could not kill them all.

He was riding past a small herd of cattle, asleep on their feet, head to tail in a group. *The cattle, Rulon. The rifle.* He checked the mule and slid off. He set the rifle against his shoulder and fired four times into the herd. Two cows thudded to the ground.

No one would forgive him now. He climbed back onto the mule and rode toward the horizon, which was beginning to brighten with the new day's light.

Rulon went on into the desert, to the cave where he had played as a boy. It sat under an outcropping of lava rock; the desert floor sloped downward and into a dark mouth surrounded by dusky gray blocks of basalt. Inside was a roomy cavern that trailed backward to an opening too narrow for anyone to pass through. When he was a boy, Rulon and his friends would crawl back as far as they could, moving on their bellies, and call into the gap to hear the echo.

Rulon unpacked his belongings and set them inside the cave. He unspooled his bedroll, laid it beside his trunk, and retrieved water from the tiny stream that cut a little notch in the basalt to the east. The morning light had filled the sky, but it was dark in the cave, and Rulon lit his lamp, casting harsh shadows on the walls. He took apart the rifle, cleaned it, and reloaded it, leaning it against the rock at the cave entrance.

I knew Rulon's mind completely. I thought of my own last days, in the mountains looming now above us. I thought of how fully I had left behind my life, my parents and my sister and my church — I could not have gone back. I had prepared to die, and had I survived, it would have been a failure. My whole life had been filling itself with the possibility of striking the ultimate mark. Even now, though I had lost my faith in God, I had not lost my faith in that. My faith in death. I could feel Rulon's mind gathering strength — he could live alone in the cave, he thought, a hermit's life, but it was not what he wanted. He wanted to go to an ultimate place, and there to end.

The sun crawled upward in the sky. The mule grazed. Spring showed on the land, green and tan and cool, and Rulon had an overwhelming eagerness to leave this wicked world and enter God's embrace. I hoped he would not be too disappointed. I wondered what would happen to him, and what would happen to me. The world rolls on and on. We cannot imagine it without us, even as we dream of death.

The crunching of cart wheels sounded across the desert. A wagon drew closer, and soon we saw a little cart and a mule, and then Brother Pope, sitting in the seat, forearms on his knees and hands holding the reins loosely, face sunk in the shadow of his hat brim. Rulon came out of the cave and stood with his rifle propped over his shoulder, squinting toward the sun. The cart passed twenty yards away, and Rulon waved briefly at Pope, who kept his eyes rigidly ahead. When he was out of sight, Rulon heard him clack at the mule, and the sound of the wheels sped up, and he knew that Pope would not be coming back alone.

Twilight settled onto the desert. Rulon made a fire outside the mouth of the cave and built a tripod with lengths of sage wood. He hung a pot over the fire and filled it with beans and water and a chunk of salt pork. Then he retreated to his bedroll in the cave and dropped into a thick, dreamless sleep.

In the morning, he awoke with a clarified mind. For the first time I could remember, he did not pray. He walked out to the pot to stir the beans and add wood to the fire. The smoke rose like a signal above the desert. Rulon considered what would remain of him, how the stories would be told. I stayed silent behind his eyes. He did not need me now.

He took a ledger and a red pencil from his pack and returned to the cave. He sat cross-legged on his bedroll and began to write, and I found myself entering a dream of my last hours on earth, and he bent to his task, writing faster and faster, and I stood in the clearing with Orin and the others as we watched for the posse. Rulon wrote, and I smelled the pine air, the mountain cold, and Rulon imagined he was leaving a testament, a scripture, a vessel to carry forth his righteousness. I heard the crunch of boots and looked into the trees, and Rulon filled the ledger with his furious red scrawl, and the posse slipped out from behind the trees, as though they were spirits of the mountains, and Rulon sharpened his pencil with a pocket knife, and I felt a blade in my side, between my ribs, and then came the sound of horses in the desert outside the cave. Rulon put down his pencil and took up his father's rifle, and I felt the blade again, a second wound, a fire in my side, and someone called, "Warren! You come out of there!" and Rulon stepped from the mouth of the cave into the desert, and the knife slipped from me, and he saw seven men on horseback, the sheriff and the bishop and five brethren, but not his father, and I tasted my blood, warm and thick in my throat, and Rulon raised his rifle and rested the sights on the bishop's gray felt hat, and I dropped to my knees, as if to pray, and Rulon tightened his finger on the trigger, and I fell to my side and tasted dust, and the bishop toppled from his horse and Rulon was filled with nausea and bliss and felt a sharp tug in his shoulder, a blossom of bright pain, and I saw my blood puddle and thicken on the earth, and Rulon's left arm hung useless, and I watched my blood and knew I was ascending, and Rulon braced the rifle against his hip with his right hand and fired, then the answering bullets tore into his chest and thigh, and he sank to his knees, as if to pray, and I dreamed of my ascension even as I knew it was a dream, and Rulon rode a wave of bliss and heard a voice, *the righteous need have no fear of death,* the words as clear as a rifleshot, coming to him in his own voice, *for it is a joy to enter the celestial kingdom, to spend eternity at the side of the Lord,* and his blood joined all the blood of the earth, and he sank toward it, we sank toward it, a cloak fell across our eyes and we soared.

Gulls

SARA MILLER WANTED TO KNOW what would happen if she said no. Just that: No. The thought terrified and thrilled her. Could she say it? Could he hear it? Ever since they'd left Nauvoo, she feared her father had lost touch with the will of the Lord. Now she was counting his sins again, as they stood in the dirt yard, as she watched him push the planer along the plank, watched the chapped top of his head, the white points of his raw knuckles. Tan curls rose and fell to the earth. *His pride,* she told herself. *His anger.* She held the plank. *He doesn't keep the Word of Wisdom.* The sun broke from the horizon, and the valley flowered between the mountain spines. All Zion was golden, Sara thought, and wasn't her father a part of that? She felt enclosed by the ambiguous messages of the Lord.

She didn't love Bishop Warren, but that did not come into it. She wanted to believe in it like her father and mother did, wanted to hear the voice of revelation for herself. *Celestial marriage.* Instead, her dreams were filled with corpse-hung trees, with frozen gray infants. Every day it took longer for the sunlight to burn away the visions. They appeared first on the Saints' long march from Nauvoo, as they filled the earth each day with corpses, real ones. Babies and old people. Fevered or frozen. They had walked for weeks and then months, and some days they traveled less than a mile, the handcarts sticking in the mud or breaking on stone, and some days they walked for miles and miles, taking turns on the handcart. The visions came to Sara almost every night, and then sometimes during the day, transforming what she saw right under the sun, turning the living into corpses, into rot. *He swears. He works on the Sabbath.* The visions came from the realms of the sacred and the profane, and if she had a part of that, couldn't she have a part in answering the proposal as well? Was she blasphemous? She was praying silently when her father barked, "Sara! Keep hold there!"

She started, then took the plank firmly in her hands, leaning forward to avoid her father's gaze. Her brown hair hung in a thick braid down her back, and large, pale freckles spread outward from the spine of her nose. Her father said, "Wake up, little sister," and when she looked at him, she saw a tight grimace under his squint. She feared him all the time now, and felt his disappointment in every glance. When she'd told him she wanted to pray over the proposal before giving Bishop Warren an answer, she had seen blood and confusion gathering under his skin. "Do you not think," he had whispered harshly, "that I have prayed on it myself?" She'd felt no spirit in her father then, sensed him only as a physical being: chapped face, tiny veins along the flare of his nostrils, small, rough hands, his livestock smell, his dying flesh. Three days passed, and Sara received no answer to her prayers. The expectations of Bishop Warren shaded every minute of every day, and she felt her father's heart darkening toward her.

Sara's mother called them for breakfast, and stood in front of the simple wood house, eyes shaded, watching them approach. Their land spread across the valley floor, yellow brown with its first wheat. In a week, the brethren would come for the reaping. As Hiram and Sara approached the house, he said, "We'll have that table done by dinner, Mother," and stepped past her. Inside, the single room was empty but for a stove and a few crude chairs. "It was starting to feel like a fast out there," he said. An edge of correction. They sat in the chairs and held bowls of sorghum mush. Hiram turned to Sara, and she was seized again by a vision—his eyes turned rank and rotten, the pupils roving wildly under a milky film, and gray flesh sloughed from his face. He asked, "What's wrong, little sister?" but she didn't answer. He was risen from the dead, not yet earth or spirit, and she wondered if the fullness she felt inside came from the Lord or from the other, and then she knew she would tell him *No*, she would tell him *I cannot*, she would tell him *It is not the Lord's will*, although she could not be certain.

Or she would not tell him anything. She would simply

leave, for she could survive anything now, she had survived everything. She had wrapped a dead child in an old dress for burial. She had touched the bodies of the dead in the morning after touching them alive the night before. She could walk to Salt Lake City and work as a laundress or climb into the mountains and pray for the Lord to provide, as he had done for Christ. She remembered the moment they reached the top of the final pass, 326 days after leaving Nauvoo, and saw where Brother Brigham had begun building a city of the Lord. She had felt illuminated from within. Her father had prayed, and as he spoke, Sara felt herself fill with light until, vibrating with energy, she was swept out of her body. She rose above them all, above Mother and Father and herself, soared over farmland, darted around circling hawks, and when she came to Salt Lake City, over those twenty or thirty buildings, those mud streets, those tiny Saints, she could tell the temple because it glowed, not with light or color but with a silent vibration that was the voice of the Lord. She returned to her body, and when she came to, she said, "The Lord has spoken to me. This is the place."

Hiram had gasped. "Do not blaspheme, little sister."

Now, over breakfast, he prayed, the words as familiar and pliant as a worn rope, incanted, *nourish and strengthen, watch and protect, O God the Eternal Father.* He thanked the Lord for his bounty, for their piece of paradise, for his protection and guidance from the constant death on the trail. His voice settled over them and Sara's confidence fled. She felt vainglorious and selfish. *Not my will but thine, Lord.*

Her father's words. And then she thought of her mother's: *None but the most righteous are called to live in the principle*. Abruptly she knew that the problem was within her own soul.

Hiram and Sara returned to the yard to finish the table, and Abby set to work inside the house. The sun was low in the sky and rising. Soon, Sara saw a man she didn't know riding from the neighboring fields, waving his hat. *This is how the world changes. A rider, a message*. His name was Brother Spencer. He spoke to her father.

"Acres and acres of 'em," he said. "Far as you look."

"Bugs?" Hiram asked.

"Monster bugs. Like nothing. Like crickets, maybe, but bigger. Big as your thumb and black."

He said the crickets had made a black carpet of the land, were marching through the crops on Brother Johansen's allotment, leaving nothing but chaff and dust.

"At this rate, they'll be here in two or three days," Brother Spencer said.

Sara knew he was scared. The Lord wasn't with him. Her father seemed calm, and as she watched him question the man, she thought again that he was steadfast and solid. *He led us through the wilderness*.

The man said they'd tried to stamp out the bugs, and still they came. They'd tried to burn them, and the crickets crawled over the husks of the dead. Sara watched him speak, his right hand gesturing over and over toward the horizon, and she suddenly saw him as bloated and rotten, reeling in his saddle, dead and foul and emptied of his soul. His curdled eyes swam aimlessly. Pink, pale fluid glistened in the tufted hair of his ears and trickled down his ashen neck. His insect tale sounded perfectly natural.

Everybody had to get down there, he was saying, voice thickened and wet. Everybody had to stop the crickets or the crops would be destroyed.

They rushed to the Johansens, Hiram drawing farther and farther ahead of Sara and his wife, shovel on a shoulder. The smaller he grew, the more Sara's love for him came back. *The mote in his eye,* she thought. *That's what you're going on about. And look at him now.* His strides ate up the land.

When Sara came to the top of the rise, she saw the unruly black floor of insects, a wave of them, spread across the Johansens' green-golden barley, a quarter mile wide. A sound made of a million small sounds. A scent of cereal dust. From above, Sara thought the mass of crickets looked like a writhing black scythe, a great blade inching through the wheat. A line of men dug a trench across the field, while another group set fire to the barley between the creatures and the trench. Sara thought of the plagues of Egypt, of reptiles falling from the heavens, blood in the water. God was punishing the Egyptians then. *And what about us?* Her father had said when they left the house, "Pray for the Lord's help, everyone. Pray for guidance."

He didn't think the bugs were sent by the Lord. How could you ever know it? How did you ever read the world with sureness? She'd heard a pamphleteer in Nauvoo three years earlier, shouting about the evils of Mormonism and plural marriage: "And I ask you, my fellow citizens, what kind of decent people live this way, bigamists raising bigamist children? They are damned before the Lord." She was twelve then, and it was the first time she understood the depth of the hatred. The Gentiles considered them indecent, offensive, doomed.

She didn't want to be wrong about that. What if that man was right? What if the insects were the army of God, sent to punish them?

She watched as her father and mother took turns at the front, watched the Saints strike at the insects with shovels and planks while walking steadily backward, watched the children rush toward the bugs and then away, like birds dancing with the soft waves of the Great Salt Lake, and then she dreamed the Saints were a battalion of corpses, blue white and frail, and they would be consumed by the insects, which would then move on to whatever new purpose their master could devise.

By the next sacrament meeting, three farms were bare. The crickets were spreading toward Bishop Warren's fields and would be into the Millers' within the week. With weariness and fear in his voice, Bishop Warren asked the Saints to fast and pray for deliverance. Watching him at the head of the ward, his eyes clasped shut, Sara thought he was a great man to take the faith of others as his own responsibility. She closed her own eyes before his face could cave and rot. She realized that, like her father, Bishop Warren did not see the devouring horde as something the Lord had sent—in asking for deliverance, he was assuming the Lord's hand was not in it. She wanted to crawl inside that idea but couldn't do it. She watched him intently as he spoke, and could feel no message from her heart.

She thought, *This is how the voice of the Lord stays silent on Earth.*

The Saints fasted for three days. At sundown, Abby served beans and pan bread. Hiram prayed and prayed, and Sara could see doubt driving him to his knees again and again. She could taste it in the air when he spoke. The Lord was not with him. But He was not with her, either.

They dug a trench along the edge of their land and filled it with wheat straw. They had little kerosene and no one had any to lend, so Hiram sprinkled it sparingly onto the spiky bed of stalks. The crickets droned less than ten yards away, their front guard hidden beneath the wheat still standing. The air filled with clatter and chaff. Sara stood rapt, staring toward the receding wheat, the stalks tipping and falling, a handful of black, horny insects clinging to each one as it toppled. The sound of them rose, a chorus of metallic chatter.

The Saints were waiting for the crickets to draw near enough to set the trench afire. Sara prayed, *Show me, show me, show me,* knowing it was a sin. She no longer even thought of Bishop Warren as a man, no longer wondered what the sheets in his home might smell like or how she might share life with her sister wife, no longer speculated about the nights in the marriage bed, his beard on her shoulder. She felt no answer anywhere in the world, no answer but God's silence.

She watched Hiram in the line of Saints along the trench, armed with shovels, and she thought he would lead them, though the flesh of his face was crumbling and gray, blotched with bruises. She felt that for all her questioning she must either follow or live a bare, unprotected life. She had seen only the dead for days now, the grins of the Saints set in bony gums, their rotten smells, their putrid masses under the thinnest skin. Sara pressed a finger to her arm. She thought *the dead don't need food, and Saints need only the Lord's nourishment.* If the insects ate it all they would discover who among them was an imposter.

Her father had stopped speaking to her. For twelve days she had refused to give an answer. Flouting God's law. She knew her father blamed her for the insects. Bishop Warren had not rescinded his proposal. He had told Hiram, while she sat silently by, "She is a serious girl, and it's good that she wants to be certain," but his smile was unconvincing. Sara wondered if he would take back his offer. She wondered if her father would love her even if he decided she was wicked.

When the crickets drew near, Hiram set fire to the trench. The flame moved in spurts and jerks, bursting when it reached the kerosene, and flickering through the rest of the straw. The front line of crickets entered the flames, marched blindly in, and began to hiss and pop, and still they came, climbing over the others to their deaths, pushing farther into the fire, until the flames began to die under the mass of them. Some of the creatures were dying but not enough. Sara trembled with thrill, because the insects were overcoming the flames, because as they died they defeated the flames and made a path for those to come, *it's a miracle,* and they were nearing the edge of the trench, *isn't it a miracle?,* and then they were at the other side and the first creature placed its spiny foot on the earth at Sara's feet, *if it isn't a miracle then what in this world, Lord, is?*

Sara knelt. She was becoming smaller, lighter, and then she was down among the insects, and the only thing in the world was the noise of them, the churn of their bodies upon one another, the clack of their black hulls, a heavenly vibration that resounded only because they were pushing in the same direction, and they were invincible. They crawled onto her legs and began eating her cotton skirt. She placed her hands down for them to crawl upon her, some of them swarming by and others stopping to chew at her clothing or hang from her skirt, and she was surrounded, feeling the scratch of their legs and the points of their antennae and their light husks. Her mind calmed, and she felt herself lifted into the air by the hand of God.

But it was simply the hand of her father. He was shouting soundlessly and beating crickets from her skirt. For the first time in days, Sara saw her father as living flesh, as vibrant and alive, and she thought that the world had been set right or her mind had been set right, and then the shouting began, all the Saints shouting and pointing, and she looked up and saw them, the encroaching flock of seagulls, filling the air with their wing rush, a froth of white against the sky, a dominion of bird noise and bug noise. Her father hugged her, lifting her off the earth. The gulls took up the insects in their beaks and devoured them, and then ate more, and when they'd had their fill they vomited the bugs and ate some more. Sara watched with dismay as the gulls scattered and destroyed the insects, broke the wave into tiny parts, took apart the miracle, and when she looked at her father, he was shouting, as though into a great wind, "We're saved, little sister, we're saved," and the Saints were jumping into the air and laughing, and some were kneeling and others embracing.

Sara looked down the long line of Saints to the end, where Bishop Warren stood, an empty shape against the earth. *There is no answer,* she thought. He lifted an arm and waved it back and forth. She knew he was waving at her. *Or at least not one for me.* There was no noise left anywhere else on earth. She had wanted to tell her father first, but she raised her hand simply in reply, and wondered as she did so if Bishop Warren understood that she was saying yes.

Diviner

FEBRUARY 27, 1825

A NEW REPORT REGARDING TREASURE.
Josaiah Stowell heard from his cousin in Damascus
the story of the Mink Gang, road agents some decades back
believed to have buried coins and bills in a strongbox along
our valley road, the spoils of a famed spree of robberies.
Stowell's cousin is a former sheriff, and the report confirms,
in some respects, other tales of which I have written here.
The stories gather and gather. They are becoming harder to
discredit. Elizabeth used to scoff at the notion — "Treasure,"
she would huff, lovely with indignation. "You men would do
anything to avoid honest labor."

Stowell called a meeting of the five landowners along the
valley bottom. Said if we throw in together, our chances im-
prove.

I say, "Dig up the whole Susquehanna Valley?"

Stowell had another notion, however. Treasure seekers. Money diggers. Spiritualists. We pitch in for expenses, give a share of any discovery.

I say, "Leave me out." Knowing they want me — and my acreage — to be a part of it.

If Elizabeth could see me now, from heaven or whatever perch a righteous Lord would grant her, she would be proud that I refused them. But if she knew my heart, she would be dismayed.

Tonight, Emma says, "I'd like to see you men split up a treasure. I would dearly love to see that."

She is enough like her mother that I am able to go on.

MARCH 8, 1825

I have tried again to pray. Five months since Elizabeth has gone, and I remain unable to find the language. I kneel and fold my hands and close my eyes, waiting to be joined by the Lord. He never comes. I have not set foot in that church since she died, and Emma has stayed away with me. But she is seeking, searching, and I feel her disappointment in me.

I fear for my soul, for I am angry at Him, and He is silent.

MARCH 13, 1825

Stowell came to see me without the others.

Says, "The others respect you, Isaac." Which is preposterous. The others do not respect me, and no one requires persuasion but me. The others are all joined in the effort, those with land between these hills — Pratt, Stoudamire, Story, Stowell — all but me.

And I possess most of it, these acres claimed by my father upon his arrival from England, cleared and cultivated, before there ever was a New York or Pennsylvania splitting up the valley. Our family's only home here since. It is itself our treasure.

I say, "What if your man comes here and tells you the treasure is on my land? If I have not joined you, what then?"

I could have been easier on him. Just told him yes — or even no, though I do not believe I will tell him no — but there is something in me that does not want to give up the advantage.

Stowell worked his hat, twisted it. I thought he might turn rash. Says, "Some of us have profited less than you, these last years. You might think of that."

I say, "Josiah, I will think of that. I will think of that indeed."

MARCH 17, 1825

Emma took me to see the traveling preacher outside Windsor today. He had a tent on the banks of the Susquehanna River, and it took us three hours in the wagon, the road thick with mud. The preacher, one Erwin Barnhill, says he is establishing a new church. The Golden Chalice of Jesus Christ. He says only those whose faith burns hot will be welcome. The lukewarm and the Sunday faithful can stick with the other churches — "They can have you, O ye of paltry faith!"

He stormed around the stage, thrusting his arms in every direction and bellowing, face red as a boil. Heels clattering the planks. Emma rapt.

Barnhill says the Lord has sent him visions of building a great empire in His name here in the valley, a place where the righteous can exclude themselves from the wicked world. The air was cool, and the tent smelled of wet canvas and horses. Barnhill's cheeks were damp and veiny. He wore new shoes of cheap, shiny leather, and his pant cuffs were frayed. At one point, he was seized, he said, with a fever for God and began to spasm and fell to the stage. Afterward, he held his head between his hands and told us in his booming voice that he had seen a vision of a golden chapel here on the banks of the river, glorious in God's light.

I saw Josaiah Stowell in the crowd up ahead and he nodded to me afterward but would not hold my eye. Caught up in the spirit, I suppose. Some of the others were there, too — Stoudamire, Pratt. People hereabouts will believe nearly anything. This Barnhill was about the five-hundredth man to come and say he is forming a church, talking about visions. It was Emma's idea to go, and after, as the wagon lurched and stuck on the road home, she asked me brightly how I had enjoyed the sermon.

"Well," I say, "it was a sight."

She didn't answer directly. The silence was fraught, but

at least the weather was pleasant and the hills were plump with spring green. At last, she says in a quiet voice, "I should think you might appreciate the chance to see a man swept up so in his faith."

"He certainly was swept up."

"I, for one, find it invigorating," she says — her final word on the bumpy ride home.

MARCH 20, 1825

I gave Josiah Stowell my answer, and we have sent for the seer. Forgive me, Elizabeth, but I must live with these men.

They say he brings a reputation from Palmyra for seeking buried treasure. I say, "Yes, but does he have a reputation for *finding* the treasure," and Stowell says, "Isaac Hale, if it was up to you, we would all sit here and starve." Which is purely foolish. None of us are near to starving. Though we are desperate, all of us, for a prosperous harvest.

I told Emma, and she asked me, "How can he find the treasure if you all cannot?

I say, "They say he uses special stones."

Emma says, "Uses them how? Is he magic?" quietly, in her way, which ordinarily makes me proud.

I say, "Daughter, you forget your place, as usual," and she says, "Fortunately, you are here to remind me."

I insist on one concession. He will stay with me, this Joseph Smith. Where I can keep him under my eye.

MARCH 25, 1825

The Pratt boy has stopped coming to the house, and I finally asked Emma about it today.

She says, "I told him to stop."

Matter-of-fact. Stirring the pot.

"Told him to stop coming to see you?"

It delights her, to see me so uncomfortable.

She says, "I told him that while I am quite fond of him as a friend — quite, quite fond, as a dear, dear friend — that I feared his intentions were otherwise, and that I couldn't in good conscience continue our dear, fond friendship without *clarifying* the terms."

And then, as though she had just thought of it, she says, "And anyway, I don't want to leave you now, Papa."

I loved to hear her say it, though it will make trouble for me with Pratt. His son is an oaf, and Emma is too smart for him by half. She has begun teaching at the school. In town, lately, the young men are like wolves around her. I watch them watch her, and wait until they catch my eye, and take pleasure to see them flinch and waver. At night, when I am in my room, when I can no longer hear her moving about her room or banging in the kitchen, I feel alone upon all the earth.

APRIL 2, 1825

Smith arrived today, at my home, having come on a stranger's wagon. The others were waiting to greet him. All of us hungry for it, greedy. Even me. The crops have been poor, and the livestock sickly, though none of us can see a reason why. My accounts have come to a thin place, and it's been worse for the others. Stowell says we are cursed until we find that treasure. Stoudamire and Story say we are cursed anyway. One time I asked them why we might be cursed, and what the treasure would have to do with that curse, and they shook their heads at me, as though I were a child.

Another time I asked whether, if we did find the treasure, and it was indeed ill-gotten gains, we shouldn't try to give it back. We were gathered around Pratt's wagon on the path.

"Give it back to who?" Pratt says, scratching madly at his leg.

"To whoever it was taken from."

"Taken from thirty-odd years ago? Or forty?"

The others laughed, and I let it go. I didn't want to give any money back either.

Joseph Smith climbed down among us and shook each hand solemnly. He is a striking figure — tall, slender, strong. He has broad shoulders and large, clean hands, and his face is boyish and handsome, with rust-colored hair sweeping upward and back from his forehead and temples, like the puffed breast of a hawk. Kept as careful as any woman's. He wore a suit of dark brown linen, with a waistcoat and a frilly tie. He shook our hands gravely, one by one, and told us he was eager to help find our spoils. His words — "our spoils."

But first, he says, "I should like to retire to my room to pray and restore my strength, for it has been a long and trying journey."

In the middle of the afternoon. After a wagon ride.

Emma and I helped him settle into the room under the stairs that her mother had used for sewing and reading. When we withdrew he shook my hand, then turned to Emma and bowed and said, "Miss Hale."

She fairly glowed. Later, in the kitchen, she said, "Fancy."

APRIL 3, 1825

Today he walked the valley alone. We gathered at my house to wait, and left the fieldwork for another day. Pratt says he spotted him kneeling in prayer in a small grove of trees. Stowell says, "They say he has a special sense for these kinds of inquiries," and Pratt says, "I feel it in him, too. I sense it," and Stowell says, "I do as well, a spirit, a light," and then there was a silence in which I did not speak and they turned to me and Stowell says, "Do not pollute this with your doubt, Hale," and I say, "I have not spoken a word against him," and Pratt says, "I have a sense about you, too, Brother Hale."

These men, these fools. My neighbors.

Emma asks me why I have agreed to go along, and to pay my portion, if I am so doubtful.

"Did I say I was?" I ask.

"Over and over again. I recall you said you believed your neighbors might be easier to gull than a child. And if I remember correctly" — she was beautiful as she spoke, flushed and quick — "you called Josaiah Stowell a preposterous old fool for throwing money after soothsayers and oracles."

Emma understands me better than anyone, ever, better than her mother, forgive me, better than my own mother. Not because she knows my doubts — everyone knows those. They read them on my face. No, what Emma understands is that I want to hear her recite them back to me.

"I *am* unbelieving," I tell her. "But doubt is not certainty, Daughter. In all things, we must prepare for the chance that we are wrong."

Do I believe this? I do not know. Emma seems to enjoy it, though. Her teasing eyes are the same brown-yellow gems as her mother's, and her hair the same shining dark brown, but she is taller, plainer. Funnier. Her birth nearly killed Elizabeth, who lost two children before, and I could never love anyone the way I love my daughter. I could not stand it.

I say, "I must live here among these men. And I would like to have my share of the treasure, too, if it turns out I am wrong."

In truth, I could not bear it if the others were to find the treasure without me, lording it over me in town and as they passed in their carts. And if the deceiver proves himself false, don't I want to be there to proclaim it? Greed and vanity, you turn the world.

He charms Emma over dinners, this Smith. He brings crocuses from the fields. He asks her questions about her students. He tells her stories of the things he has found in other places, Indian treasure and silver mines, and I can tell his stories amuse her. They very nearly amuse me. I tell myself she doesn't believe him, that she is too wise to believe this pretender, and that she looks at me, bright in the eyes, only so we may share our disbelief.

APRIL 7, 1825

He has been reading the stones for two days now. I cannot quite believe it. That we are paying him to do this. He puts the stones — two opaque, dirty yellow oblongs, like the eggs of a strange, small bird — into his hat, and places his face into the hat. He says the stones emit light and visions.

He reels around, as though being buffeted by great winds. Sometimes he moans, and other times he spouts gibberish. Pratt whispers, "Tongues!" Smith stops and sits on the ground, acts exhausted, places his face in his hands, kneels to pray, and walks away from us, muttering. And then — more face in the hat!

I was certain this would be the end of all this nonsense. The others would see him as did I, and we would put a halt to it. But when he began and I looked to the others, Stowell looked back ashen faced, moved, Pratt's eyes were round, as though he were witnessing a faith healing, and Stoudamire pulled on the brim of his hat and shrugged. We do not live in the same world, my neighbors and I. They live in a world of codes and secrets and the hope that all will be understood, and I live in the world where bafflement and mystery are but the foundation and the condition. I felt it even before Elizabeth's passing, and it has only grown. No light shines through any stone.

When Smith told us at last, after two days of face-in-the-hat and wringing his hands and muttering from his room at night, that he had found the spot, the others were ecstatic. He led us back to the poplar grove that spills from a draw in the low hills crossing from Stowell's property to Pratt's.

"The treasure lies within that grove," he announced.

Pratt says, "Can you be any more specific?"

Stowell, like a lump, scratched his beard. "We'll have to get up a work party."

Smith says, "The visions are coming strong now, fast, and I can't be more precise. I must read them more and pray on them. All I see is that it lies to the side of a small bunch of trees, three trees in a close triangle, two larger and one smaller, and that the treasure lies beneath an open place to the west of the three trees. It is in a large box or trunk."

As he spoke, he kept his eyes closed, as though he were viewing the place in his mind. He spoke as one who has always been believed, and who does not doubt that he will continue to be so.

Pratt says, "So, I guess, a work party. Get some shovels and some strong backs."

I say, "That's a good half acre."

Pratt doesn't look at me. Stowell does, though — hard, a warning — but says only, "We'll have to find the right spots. The spots that match."

I say, "Match?"

Pratt says, "You can decamp any time you like, Hale. Nobody would miss you one bit."

Now that my land's not in it. I say, "Not in your lifetime."

Smith smiled broadly at Pratt, and then at me, and then at Pratt again, the big, horsey smile of a man prepared for a challenge.

"Brother Pratt," he says. "It is no sin to doubt, and we should not blame our brethren if their faith falls short in difficult times."

He put his hand on my shoulder. Then adds: "Within reason."

Him! Speaking of reason!

That night, over her good beef stew, Emma says to the diviner, "And have you made my father a rich man yet, Mister Smith?"

She has no notion of his ways, and I cannot bring myself to describe them to her.

He says, "Your father, Miss Hale, is a wealthy man already," and she blushed for the first time I ever saw. After, he helped her clear the table and wash the dishes. I sat in the parlor and listened. Soon, I heard the murmuring change and increase, and I realized that Smith was singing—first "Billy Boy" then "Come Here, Fellow Servant"—and gradually I heard Emma's voice join his.

APRIL 10, 1825

A Saturday. Pratt and Stoudamire walked the grove with Smith, looking for combinations of trees and stone, and set men to digging in small teams. They tried four places with no success, and Smith walked beside, muttering and consulting the hat. Smith and I keep about the same pace with the shovel. I will not break my back for this.

Emma made a lunch for us, pushing a handcart laden with bread and cheese and apple cider. She looked at me briefly, standing at the edge of all that work, and frowned. Or perhaps simply failed to smile.

Smith was first to the cart, and I could not tell whether Emma was blushing or flushed from exertion. The sight of them, him joking, her laughing, made me hunger for his failure all the more.

After lunch, Emma left. More face-in-the-hat. Smith says the visions are getting stronger. He says tomorrow, we should move to a spot toward the back of the grove. He says he is seeing it more clearly now.

APRIL 11, 1825

The men have dug up half the valley, it seems. By midday, Smith took a new tack: The treasure is sinking, he says. "I fear there is an enchantment upon it." He says he does not understand why the Lord is keeping the treasure from us, but he puts his face in his hat and says he can see the treasure, just there, no there, under that mound, dig faster men, you must dig faster — and still the men, these fools, follow.

At night, we do not speak, neither Smith nor Emma nor me. Over dinner, he exerts his image: weary, baffled, dejected, yet resolute. He rests his face in his hands. He casts these impressions of himself outward, like a conjurer, and I am certain he is not to be believed. I shoved his plate at him, and it scraped upon the table, and he and Emma both reddened. Smith took his plate and rearranged it and ate in silence.

APRIL 13, 1825

My amusement has worn away, and I have grown weary. It is time to get into my fields and begin breaking the earth, and yet here we are.

The men dug for most of the morning. The grumbling was general and growing hotter. Smith stood beside them, placing the hat to his face, and then removing it to provide new reports. His hair flew loose about his head, and his cheeks flushed pink. He could not understand why the Lord was causing the treasure to sink, he said — reminding me of a preacher whose passion and intensity peak in the moments where belief might most be strained — but he was seeing it, he assured us.

Pratt broke first. He stumped over to Smith and pushed his shovel at him. Says, "I think it's time you took a turn." That wet hiss. Tobacco blackening the corners of his mouth, muddying his words. Says, "Might help out your fortune-telling abilities."

Smith put his shoulders back. You get the sense he likes this manner of discourse. The challenge. Says, "I am not afraid of labor, Brother Pratt. But I hope you will not take it amiss if I suggest that it is not for a lack of strong backs that our mission here is being thwarted."

Stowell took three steps toward Smith and says, "Maybe you ought to tell us what strength it is we're lacking."

Smith turned his eyes from man to man. Says, "Faith. Doubt has been sown among you, and it is preventing us from reaching our reward."

Pratt, Stowell, Story — all turn to me. Stoudamire *spits* toward me, a brown sluice that contracts in the dust like a worm. The others cross their forearms on their shovels. Pratt glares with pure hatred. He's been telling the others that Emma backed out on his boy, broke her word, and suggesting something improper between Emma and Smith.

I say, "Between the faithful and the doubters, one of us has so far been correct."

Smith says, "I do not name any one man. I see an erosion of faith that is general."

He smiled at me when he said this. It sometimes feels as if we have a perfect understanding, he and I. Pratt, still glaring at me, says, "Maybe you ought to just leave anyway. You ain't helping any."

I say, "I'm a partner here same as you, Francis."

He hates his given name.

Pratt says, "I'll buy you out right now."

I say, "The price has doubled." He threw his shovel to the earth and started toward me, then let the others catch him.

I say, "The Lord does not love a coward, Francis."

Smith stepped in. He asked us to leave him alone to pray, and he went off over the hill and was gone for more than an hour. We ate our lunches, sat on the earth, and talked.

I sat with Stowell. He says, "You ought to leave Pratt alone."

I say, "I'm waiting for him to say one word to me about my girl. One word."

"Let that go."

"I will not."

"He's a fool."

"You're all fools, Josaiah."

Smith returned. He says he has seen a clearer vision than before, and he directed the men to the place. A swollen lump on the hillside, a little above and west of the most recent digging. Smith says, "I see it here clearly, brothers. I feel it more strongly than before."

The men dug and dug, and the dirt was soft there, thick and brown. The odor of fresh dirt and greening lent an atmosphere of hope. The sun speckled down through the forest in shafts and beams, and turned the leaves bright green. I found myself swept up with sensation, emotion, memory — this place, this new season, this new country, the land my father had journeyed to. My home, Emma's home. This foolishness would soon be over, and life would resume, and I would have a satisfaction to carry silently all my days.

Soon Stoudamire and two others were nearly to their waists in the earth. Smith and I stood below, watching. He seemed placid. The thought sped through my mind that he

believed all this. That he was sincere. Which was no comfort.

The men dug and dug. Smith spent more time with his
face in the hat. I wondered if my father was someplace
where he could see me, and what he must think. I wondered
if Elizabeth could see me. She must feel that I have fallen,
that I have landed among vain, greedy men, diviners and
charlatans. And she is right.

Toward twilight, and still no treasure. Smith told the
men he saw the treasure sinking again, and he knew not
why. Says, "This is not easy, my brothers. These signs and
visions do not come simply. This enchantment has me be-
wildered."

I say, "I'll wager." Eyes on Pratt.

The day ended, no treasure. Hillside covered with holes,
piles. The men grumbled, sore at heart, and I had a hard
time pleasuring in the failure. Had I fooled myself? Allowed
myself to hope? The possibility makes me ashamed. I wonder what Elizabeth would say to me, were she here. I hear
the words she said to me on countless Sabbaths, as I criti-
cized her glib, chatty pastor. *Your heart is not as hard as you
pretend.*

As the men wandered off in the twilight, Smith called to
them, urged them to keep heart. Says, "It is always darkest
before the dawn, brothers. Keep that in your hearts as you
pray tonight."

Some of them stopped, and turned. Looked at him with
no charity.

Pratt says, "I think a fair man would consider some recompense for services unrendered."

Smith nodded, prepared. Says, "Now, Brother Pratt, my understanding was that the retainer was for expenses incurred in my travel and for my board and food, and the like. I said at the outset that I could make no guarantees. I do not understand these visions, do not understand what makes them come and go, do not understand the way the world and the will of the Lord come together. I try my best. I do my best, you men, and dare any one of you to say different."

Everyone but Pratt turned from him. Would not look.

And Smith says, "But if you ask it of me, I will give it. I will return the money you have paid, and suffer the loss as part of the price of settling any hardness in your heart toward me, which I could not bear."

Smith beamed at that. The men could not ask for the money back, if he was so willing to give it. And though he is a fraud, I cannot help but acknowledge a truth: He is right. That was our agreement.

Pratt told Smith to leave us, and we talked there as the darkness arrived. Stowell finally says, "I'm nearly done with this," and the others agreed.

Stoudamire says, "I feel just stupid," and Pratt glared at me.

I shrugged. I was surprised to find no pleasure in it.

Later, as I prepared for bed, I heard murmuring on the porch, and when I came to the door, I found them kneeling together in the lilac-scented night air, Smith praying for the Lord to ease Emma's grief over the loss of her mother. Emma's eyes were closed tightly, and on her lovely face was a look I can only describe as joyful. Brightened from within. Smith's voice a low melody.

APRIL 14, 1825

Last evening, after I had written here, there were events of much import.

In the middle of the night, there came a clamorous knocking below and a shouting in the front yard. Voices calling, "Imposter! Diviner! Come out! Come out!" I came down to the door, and found Emma and Smith already there, whispering. Emma's color high. She says, "Father, we must help him."

I say, "You reap what you sow, Daughter."

"You must not stand with them. Whatever you think, you cannot stand with them."

Outside, they were shouting, "Hale! Hale! Turn him over!"

Smith stayed silent. His eyes were calm, moving around the house methodically as if seeking a hidden egress.

I went into the yard. The flames in the lanterns jumped and wavered, cleaving the faces with light and shadow. Two men held large burlap sacks that seemed weightless. Stowell held the flame of his lantern under a pot of pitch.

I say, "What do you men want?"

"We want what's proper."

The story spilled out of them, as if in chorus. Stoudamire had gotten a letter that afternoon from his brother in Palmyra. Smith had accepted a retainer there, and when the treasure failed to materialize, he had told them the same things he had been telling us — the treasure was sinking. Keep digging. Then, he promised to return some of the money they had paid, but instead left under cover of night. The man who put Smith up in his home reported that several items had gone missing, including pieces of silver and an emerald cravat pin, which some of the men here later swore they had seen him wear.

Despite myself, I could not imagine him a common thief.

A voice says, "Stand aside, Hale."

I don't know if it was the shadows or the angle of light or if some spirit or demon has hidden them in darkness, but I could not tell who was speaking.

"So you can become murderers?"

"Nobody's getting murdered."

It sounded like Pratt, like his muddy hiss. I considered going for my flintlock, but could not imagine using it against these men, my neighbors, regardless. They clamored in and seized Smith by the arms and legs, and carried him out as Emma protested. They hauled him into the yard, and stretched him upon the ground.

"You will learn your lesson tonight, you devil," a voice from the mob says. They tore his shirt from him, and began to daub the tar on with gummy brushes. He writhed and cried out, the pitch sticking and smearing, blackening his white skin in the torchlight. Pratt tried to stuff a tar brush in Smith's mouth. Says, "I'm having a vision of you eating some tar, you bastard. Eat it, damn you." But Smith twisted and kept his mouth away, though gobs of the black stuff stuck to his cheeks and hair. Smith cries, "Lord, Lord, spare me," and a voice says, "He ain't gonna help you, sharp."

They covered him in white down, and formed a circle as he tried to flee, kicking him and pushing him back in. It was sickening to watch, though Smith was guilty of everything they said. He deserved it all. Pratt gave him a hard kick in the side and Smith dropped to his knees, holding his ribs, covered with pitch and clumps of white feathers, no longer so grand, and Pratt gave him another kick, and he moans again: "Lord, spare me." It was sickening to watch, and it was sickening that all I did was watch, until Emma, weeping beside me, whispers, "Father, will you do nothing?"

By then, it was easy to chase the men away, and we helped Smith back inside. The tar was cooling, sticking. I got him to his room, where Emma threw an old blanket over the bed, and Smith eased down onto it, taking shallow breaths.

Emma brought a stiff rag, a basin and a bottle of camphor oil. It took her hours, picking and scrubbing, pausing when the pain became too much for him, and sometimes wincing in anticipation herself.

Smith's skin was all raw welts, bruises, and blisters. Strands of pitch lined his cheek, growing outward like the legs of a spider from a black ball on his neck. He was mostly quiet, and took the worst of it well. I begrudge to admire him, but cannot help it.

Once, he whispers, "Emma, I swear, you are an angel, sent to me by the Lord," and the blood rushed upward from her neck and buried itself under her hairline.

It was dawn before he was cleaned up. I stayed in that room and watched and said little. It was hard to hate him, like that, though I kept feeling I should.

I tell him, "You can stay here a couple days to rest up, but you better move along as soon as you can."

He says, "Of course. Thank you, Brother Hale."

I say, "Keep your brothers."

Later, I took the wagon into Harmony Township for bandages and supplies. I passed Stoudamire out in his field, behind a team, and wondered how I should greet him now. I raised a hand, and he didn't raise one back, though I saw his head turning to follow me as I passed, eyes sunk in shadow. In town, people's eyes slid away from me. Joe Banks, the general merchant, the yappiest dog in the valley, greeted me with a grunt. Two women from Elizabeth's church turned from me so quickly they must have injured their necks.

He is ours now.

When I returned, Emma was sitting beside him as he slept.

I tried again to pray. How shall I understand your world when it becomes absurd, O Lord? I imagined Elizabeth looking down on me — she would have nothing but rebuke for the fact that I helped bring Smith here, and would have called out my true reasons: greed, weak will, meanness. But she would have liked this, that we cared for him, though she would have known as well that it was Emma's doing.

When he goes, all will be better. All will be restored.

MAY 21, 1825

A long silence. We have started planting the back field in wheat, the seed on loan from Pratt, of all people. He couldn't wait to do it. Hauled it over himself and sat there while I unloaded it with my new man. He said nothing of that night. I have seen the others only in passing, and no one has spoken of it. It has been erased.

Our accounts in town have fallen into arrears. Everything rides on this crop.

Smith has left us, and yet he returns on occasion. He has been seen in town. He preached to a gathering in Afton about the corruption of the churches, about the Lord's disappointment in his supposed servants on earth.

I say to Emma, "That man has more nerve than sense."

She says, "You used to admire nerve."

"No, ma'am. The worst of us are full of nerve. Any fraud you name."

She was rolling out dough for biscuits, and at this she started rolling harder. I was sitting in the chair at the kitchen table. A glass of milk before me.

I say, "The one thing you might credit him with is industry."

"I should think you might credit him with kindness. Bravery, to return here. Faithfulness."

"Oh, Daughter."

"Is there no one in this world who is not a fool to you?"

She was right. I have hardened my heart in every direction. The man who despises all others is lost, and I despise all, all but Emma.

I say, "There must be someone, somewhere."

She paused for a long time. Says, "He is starting a church."

At this, and all it meant, I could not speak. I left the room and did not come down for dinner.

She has seen him. She is seeing him.

MAY 23, 1825

As we were scattering seed over the last of the acreage today, I looked up and there was Smith, striding at me across the broken earth. Sun at his back, so I could not read his face. In his shirtsleeves, cuffs rolled up.

I stopped, a handful of wheat kernels dusty in my palm. He waved at me, and as he drew closer, calls, "Hello, Brother Hale."

I did not answer. Shaded my eyes with a hand. He made a black shape against the dusty light.

"I wondered if you could use a hand out here."

A voice of good cheer.

I say, "I believe we have the help we need." Though there are just the four of us hand seeding this land: Jorgenson's two sons, my hired man, and myself. Once we've sowed the wheat, some fifty acres await the barley seed. I say, "I would not have figured you for farm work."

"I've done some of everything. Why don't you let me help?"

"I think I'm full up on your help."

I wished to see his reaction, but could not.

"I owe you a great debt."

"Maybe I don't want it settled."

I nodded at the others, and we started again, fanning seed into the open black soil. He watched us as we went, and I finally heard his steps across the field.

He would not have known where to find me on his own.

MAY 25, 1825

He returned today. Dressed in a new suit, a shirt of surpassing whiteness. Emma at his side, in her church dress and hair newly braided and a blush all about her.

There was no mystery in their visit. My heart blazed with anger. Smith smiled at me like a saint, just as he smiled at us all in the fields this spring. Oh! Emma. She is too clever for this. He will ruin her. I have taken once more to praying, but without hope.

He smelled of toilet water, hair combed and held in some kind of knot at the back, and when he smiled at me there was something reptilian in it that I believed only I was capable of seeing, something carefully ordered and tended and managed and false. They sat at the ends of the couch, and I sat in the chair opposite, and the thick ray of late daylight from the kitchen window filled with twirling dust and golden motes, a slice of dirty sunshine in the gloom. Smith chattered about the planting, about his plans to start a church, about the weather.

Finally, I put it to him.

"Why have you come?"

"Why, Brother Hale, I thought you might have guessed."

"Why, Smith?"

Thinking: I brought him here. I visited this upon myself.

Smith says, "I would like to respectfully ask you for your beautiful daughter Emma's hand in marriage."

"Impossible."

Emma says, "Father, please."

"Out of the question."

I fear I lost control. My voice rose in anger. I forgot myself. A flame rose in Emma's cheeks, and I saw that she faulted me for this. That she had chosen. I stood and shouted, hurled the lamp at Smith, Elizabeth's lamp with the hanging crystals, and as it shattered behind his head, upon the wall, I saw with some paltry satisfaction that he had stopped smiling.

Emma says, "Father, you are being ridiculous."

I shout, "You will never marry this man."

I shout, "I will kill you with my bare hands first."

That last, I was speaking to Smith. I believe I was looking at him when I said it.

He left, and she stayed.

I am praying, praying.

I am bereft.

MAY 26, 1825

She will not speak. She brought me porridge for breakfast, a puddle of cream on top, and when I thanked her, she did not speak. I told her I was leaving for the fields, and she did not speak. When I told her the dinner she prepared was delicious, she did not speak, and later, finally, when I sought her forgiveness, when I said, "I was not speaking to you, Daughter, I did not mean you, of course I did not mean you," she did not speak or look at me or raise her eyes from her lap.

MAY 27, 1825

It is as I feared. Of course. I do not know where they have gone. I would rather have followed her to the grave. I would rather he had choked me with his stones.

SEPTEMBER 23, 1825

There is much news.

For weeks after they left, I found myself unable to work the farm. I fell behind. I planted late, and left the north field untouched. A waste. A sin. Each day I woke well after the sun was up, and left the fields early. I didn't take on a man, and when I saw the first of the black point in the wheat, I let it spread. The crop was lost, and I could hardly care. At night, each night, the house closed around me like a tomb. I stopped shaving, rarely bathed. Filth overtook the kitchen, grime dimmed the windows. I heard mice scratching in the walls and cupboards, at all hours.

If only Elizabeth had still been with me, I might have accepted it and let Emma go. Perhaps. Perhaps. The thought of her out there, somewhere, with him — it scoured at my bones, clamored through my sleep. I imagined myself finding him someday, and wielding a tar brush or worse. I came to see him as the worst kind of evil — the smiling kind, the kind no one can recognize. If the devil himself were to come to my farm, wouldn't he come like Smith? With a handsome face and a pocket full of lovely lies? And wouldn't he leave with my daughter?

She wrote me last month. At last. Told me they had set up near Palmyra. Asked about a visit. I wrote her back and told her she was welcome to come home. Without him. She answered me: "I will come with my husband or not at all, Father."

And so I wrote her back and she came, because I was alone, alone upon all the earth, and because what I believe and what Emma believes and what Smith believes, however foolish — and what Elizabeth believed, especially that — simply does not matter. We could believe in anything at all. We might as well.

Forgive me, Elizabeth. But I no longer wonder if you are there.

I have moved in with Emma and Joseph, sold the farm and taken a room in the back of their home. At dinner, he sits at the head of the table, with a straight back and his hands in his lap, until I have joined them, and then he bows his head to pray, and when he does so I can no longer see him as the devil. He believes his foolishness, every bit of it, and so is merely a man. He never asks anyone else to pray, and I am relieved not to do it and offended not to be asked. When Emma looks at him in admiration or love or whatever it is that pulls them toward each other, I feel I have crossed into a fresh hell. And yet I am happy to be here, somewhat. I had rather be near her than not.

Acknowledgments

These stories and this book would not exist without the collaboration, guidance, and high expectations of three excellent editors: Sam Ligon, Ben George, and Ed Park. Several other readers, friends and editors, have provided invaluable help: Michael Baccam, Stephen Knezovich, Dan Vice, Pete Sheehy, Jessica Halliday, Gregory Spatz, Jordan Bass, Jill Meyers, Tonaya Thompson, and the late Jeanne Leiby. I am beyond fortunate to have Renée Zuckerbrot as my agent; every writer should have such an advocate. Particular thanks to my mother, Mary Jane Bodily, my brothers and sisters, and above all, my wife, Amy Cabe.